SOME COFFEE TO CALM THE NERVES

Nancy began taking out the ingredients for the biscuits, measuring them into a big green-glazed bowl with a chipped rim. Once there had been a set of them, all glazed in green, all perfect. They had been her mother's. This was the lone survivor.

"What did you do to make the sheriff come chasing after you?" she asked.

"Robbed the bank," Cash replied, a little too proudly. "Didn't you hear?"

"Perhaps I did," she said, sliding the coffeepot off the hearth and dumping out the grounds. "There's a lot to keep track of lately. Is this something you do often, robbing banks?"

"No, ma'am," he said from behind her. "My first time."

"Doesn't seem to me that you're too good at it, my laddie," she said, rinsing out the pot. "I'd look into another line of work, if I were you."

"Ma'am?"

His voice was suddenly too close. She spun around, knocking over the coffeepot, to find him standing only a foot away and pointing her own gun at her heart. . . .

Titles by Wolf MacKenna

DUST RIDERS
GUNNING FOR REGRET

GUNNING
FOR REGRET

WOLF MacKENNA

B

BERKLEY BOOKS, NEW YORK

GUNNING FOR REGRET

A Berkley Book / published by arrangement with
the author

PRINTING HISTORY
Berkley edition / March 2001

The Penguin Putnam Inc. World Wide Web site address is
http://www.penguinputnam.com

ISBN: 0-425-17880-3

BERKLEY®
Berkley Books are published by The Berkley Publishing Group, a division of Penguin Putnam Inc., 375 Hudson Street, New York, New York 10014.
BERKLEY and the "B" design
are trademarks belonging to Penguin Putnam Inc.

PRINTED IN THE UNITED STATES OF AMERICA

10 9 8 7 6 5 4 3 2 1

1

Dix Granger had yet to hit fifty, but just at that moment, with the storm-muted afternoon sun slanting across his craggy features, he looked like he was pushing sixty. Arizona did that to a man, Yancy Wade thought as he and Dix ambled slowly through the low, scrabbly, wind-blown growth on the canyon floor, looking for a trail that Yancy was solid sure they weren't going to find.

That picture of Dix hadn't been just a trick of the sun or the wind. To Yancy, Dix looked old at night and in the morning, too. He looked, in fact, like he'd been tunneling for ore and using his face for the shovel and pick. His dark hair was only marginally shot through with gray, but deep wrinkles bracketed his mouth and his deep blue eyes and cut furrows into the tanned leather hide of his neck and cheeks.

He didn't see so well, either, and he refused to wear glasses. That griped Yancy no end, for he knew Dix figured wearing specs would be admitting not a flaw so much as a weakness. Just plain silly, if you asked Yancy, but that was Dix. Silly, and mule-stubborn. As it was, Dix had squinted for so many years that when he slept and the wrinkles relaxed, white lines of secret flesh spun out from his eyes like spiderwebs.

Yancy figured that he'd go all spidery in the eyes, too, if he waited around long enough. Too much beating sun scorching his body, too many heat shimmers in the distance. Too many dry howlers, like the ongoing storm that had quieted some during the day, but which was gathering again, gearing up to beat more gravel and grit into his face. It made a fellow dizzy. It could kill him, in fact.

And that was before a man started tallying up the stickup artists and *bandidos* and thimble-riggers and shootists and back-stabbers that were around practically every rock. Sooner or later, the worst ones headed for the wild places, and that meant Arizona Territory.

Yancy supposed that when you were in the law business, the scare factor alone could put years on you.

Dix was the town sheriff twenty-some miles north, up in Gushing Rain, Arizona Territory. Gushing Rain was south of the Gila in the Estrella Mountains, and it was a place Yancy figured had to have been christened by either a certified optimist or a certified lunatic, because it by God sure wasn't rainy, gushing or otherwise. It was a sleepy little silver mining town—no big strikes, just slow and steady dusty production—where not much ever happened.

Well, that wasn't exactly true. Yancy, who at twenty-seven was more than two decades younger than Dix, and who had signed on as Dix's deputy two years earlier, had been shot exactly three times since Dix swore him in: once in the arm, once in the shoulder, and once in a place he'd rather not think about.

He'd also been beaten up twice, although one of those

beatings—by far, the lighter of the two—had come from Dix, himself.

He supposed he'd deserved it, after that stupid stunt he'd pulled. He'd never pop up in Dix's line of fire again, that was for sure! Dix had shot him square in the backside, and then, when he realized his deputy wasn't dead, Dix had punched him in the jaw for pulling such a jackass stunt.

Yancy wasn't sure which was worse: the .44 slug in his sitting parts or the broken jaw. He hadn't let it happen again, though, no sir, and the two of them had brought in Frank Wheeler.

Well, actually, Dix had brought in the both of them, slung over their saddles like a couple of feed sacks with legs. But where Frank Wheeler went straight to the undertaker's and into a pine box, Yancy spent the next few days flat on his stomach, and the two weeks after that sitting on a pillow.

It had been embarrassing as hell. Frustrating, too, particularly so because Doc Fedderson had wired his dad-blasted teeth shut on account of the busted jaw, and he couldn't even talk back to the wags that teased him, let alone chew solid food.

Talking back—and eating—were Yancy's strong suits.

Dix, who was currently about forty feet out and searching the ground off Yancy's right shoulder, whoaed up his horse and leaned down toward a hummock of brush.

Yancy stopped, too. "Got somethin' over there, Dix?" he asked over the low whine of the wind.

Dix sat up straight in the saddle again. "Looks like."

That was all he said and, as usual, Yancy had to prod him for details. "Well, what is it?" he asked.

Dix didn't answer, just leaned over again and stared at the ground. He shook his head.

"Line of Injun ponies pass through?" Yancy asked conversationally, shifting his weight in the saddle. He figured somebody should talk, and he was the only one willing. "Shod horses, Dix? Circus wagon? Mex bandits? Antelope? Elephant? Quail track? Dove shit?"

"You're a card, Yancy," Dix said dryly, and got down off his horse. He bent over and lifted a branch. It came away in his hand easily, with no sound other than a little swish and crackle of leaves against leaves, barely heard over the wind. Now that Yancy looked closer, he could tell that the leaves were browning on their thorny stems. Somebody had cut that brush and piled it up.

"Aw, crud," he said under his breath, and reined his bay toward Dix's sorrel. "What is it?"

Dix stood up. "Malone's horse, I reckon."

The brush explained why they hadn't seen any buzzards. "It dead?"

Dix swung back up into the saddle. "No, it just laid down for a nap and decided to tuck itself in with hopseed and creosote," he said dryly. He took out his spyglass and began to scout the canyon's perimeter.

"Funny," said Yancy, who'd just been trying to make conversation.

"Didn't mean to be," said Dix.

Cash Malone was on foot now, and he could be just about anyplace. He'd robbed the bank in Gushing Rain the day before, and Dix and Yancy had tracked him just fine up until last night.

But then the wind had come up and it blew and it blew, adding another year to Dix's features and forcing grit and grime into every crevice in Yancy's body. And any trace of Cash Malone's trail had blown south, to Mexico.

This morning, Yancy had been ready to head back to town. There was no trail to follow, after all, and they could have been back in Gushing Rain in time for supper. He could practically smell the beefsteak and fried onions at

Kendall's Café. Mrs. Kendall could char a slab of beef like nobody else. Maybe she would've made a few dried-apple pies, too. His mouth suddenly gushed saliva, and he swallowed.

But Dix? Not Dix. He wouldn't have any of it. The peckerwood never took the easy—or sensible—way out of anything. Which was why they were still out here, still headed in the opposite direction from town, going farther and farther south while Yancy got farther and farther away from that steak and dried-apple pie.

"What you tryin' to do?" he muttered too softly for Dix to hear. "Give me the rickets?"

The wind had been soft and fairly steady all day, just enough to erase all but the most sheltered track, but now it was picking up again, getting ready for another mean blow. Clouds the color of dirty nickel had moved in to blanket the skies. A wind-blown piece of brush stung Yancy's cheek, and he swore under his breath. Now he was going to have to spend another night huddled in his blanket and cowering behind a rock, listening to a dry storm howl and bitch and thunder.

His head jerked when Dix said, "Got him," and collapsed his spyglass with a heavy click.

Leave it to Dix to find a gol-darned needle in the hayloft.

"I'll be damned," Yancy muttered.

If Dix heard him, he gave no sign, only urged his gelding into a slow lope down the canyon. Yancy followed, the wind pushing at his back.

Now, frankly, he didn't expect Cash Malone to offer much resistance. He was just a kid, after all, and a piss-poor excuse for an outlaw if ever there was one. He'd struck the bank on the exact wrong day, when the silver shipment had just gone out and the time lock on the safe had secured most of the town's money. He'd only made off with fifty-some dollars from the teller's cash drawer, which was why Dix and Yancy were not exactly overwhelmed with posse.

In fact, nobody in town had been real upset. Yancy supposed the folks just figured Cash could have the money. He'd had hard times lately, and most everybody liked him. Everybody except Old Man Peterson, that was, and Old Man Peterson owned the bank.

They hadn't ridden far before Yancy began to make out what he supposed was Cash Malone. He went from a distant red speck to a running man in a red-checkered shirt pretty fast, though, and he didn't stop until Dix rode up beside him, leaned over, and grabbed a fistful of shirt.

Yancy stopped, too, but stayed back about ten paces. He had his Peacemaker out and leveled. Cash Malone was just a kid, and he was well-liked in town, as had been his ma and pa and baby sister before the smallpox took them. Cash probably wouldn't hurt a fly—at least, he hadn't hurt anybody at the bank, and had said, "Thank you, Mr. Peabody" to the teller, real polite—but a man couldn't be too careful. At least, that's what Dix kept hammering into him.

"Quit it, Cash!" Dix was shouting over the wind. It had come up a good bit in just the last few minutes. "You're caught! Just hold still!"

"Dang it, anyhow, Sheriff Granger!" Cash panted. He was played out but still trying. "Dang it! I got no luck at all!"

"Quit jerkin' around!" said Dix. The boy was flopping like a catfish on the line.

"Aw, let him go, Dix," offered Yancy. "He's about to fall down, anyhow."

Dix let loose of the boy's collar, and Cash staggered back a couple feet before the wind pushed him over sideways into a weary sit. He stayed where he plopped, his chest heaving.

"Hands on top'a your head, boy," Dix said over the blow as he stepped down. The wind was flipping his hat brim every which way, and he was holding it on with one hand. As was Cash. Yancy supposed the order had been more habit than anything else, but Cash brought his other hand up anyway and planted it atop his hat.

Dix relieved him of an old Smith & Wesson pistol while Yancy watched, and then he pulled the boy to his feet and dragged him over to his horse. He looped his rope around Cash's waist.

Neither Cash nor Dix spoke. Yancy was full of questions, though, like what the hell were they going to do now, with this wind whipping up mean, like a bag full of badgers? But he kept his lips pressed tight together and his questions to himself, mostly to avoid taking in a mouthful of dust and grit.

When Dix remounted and motioned the prisoner out ahead of him at a march, Yancy tugged his bandanna up over his mouth and nose and silently followed.

Dix was going south again, farther away from Gushing Rain. Well, maybe Dix knew a place they could hole up, Yancy thought. In all of the time he'd deputied for Dix, he hadn't been down this way. Well, he'd been south of town, all right, but never this far. And this canyon was a new one on him. But Dix knew this part of the country like the back of his hand, and he probably knew a nice, snug cave.

Yancy closed the distance and rode off Dix's near side, one hand on his reins, one hand clamping his hat to his head, hoping for the best.

But within fifteen minutes, the sky had gone so dirty yellow and so dark—and the air was so full of stinging dirt and gravel and blowing brush—that he could barely see fifteen feet in front of himself. And poor Cash was on foot, up ahead on Dix's tether line, trying to fight the wind. He was bobbing and weaving so much that he looked for all the world like a cork float with a great big fish teasing at it.

Yancy brought his horse closer to Dix's flank and shouted, "Cash Malone might have stole fifty dollars, but it don't seem to me that he deserves to get blown to hell and gone for it and take two officers of the law along for company!"

Dix looked over and mouthed "What?" at him.

Yancy tried yelling louder. "You got a destination in mind?"

They both pulled up, for Cash had fallen. While he struggled against the wind to regain his feet, Dix shouted, "Give over your guns!"

It was Yancy's turn to shout, "What?" He couldn't have heard Dix right.

But Dix slapped his holster and shouted "Guns!" again and motioned to Cash, and Yancy finally figured out what he wanted.

Yancy handed over his Peacemaker and his rifle. Then, the wind howling in his ears, he eased his horse a few feet ahead. He leaned over toward Cash Malone and through his bandanna, shouted, "Take your rope off!"

Cash looked at him quizzically, and Yancy jabbed a finger toward the rope. "Off!" he yelled again. "Take it off and climb up!"

Cash worked the knot free, and behind them, Dix reeled in his rope while Cash shoved a foot in Yancy's stirrup and climbed aboard.

"See what a mess you got us into?" Yancy called over his shoulder. "Nice kid like you, sticking up Old Man Peterson's bank! You're barely eighteen! Got your whole life ahead!"

Cash made no answer.

"Just don't go tryin' nothin' funny," Yancy continued. He could hardly hear himself for the wind. It milked tears from his eyes, filled them with dust, then blew them away. "Dix is watchin', and he's armed enough for three men!"

"Where we goin', Deputy Wade?" Cash shouted back at him as they began to move once more through an afternoon that had become as black as night, an impossible afternoon full of the howl of harsh, roaring wind and pelting grit and gravel and twigs.

"A place Dix knows," Yancy called back. At least, he hoped Dix knew where in tarnation he was leading them.

It looked to Yancy like they were going straight into the mouth of hell.

2

They plodded slowly onward, their horses' heads low. The howling wind eddied around every hillock and rock with a whistle or a moan, that being the nature of the storm. Sometimes the blast came from the side, a wall of wind that hit them with a loud rush, and they had to rein their staggering horses into a turn just to hold a straight course.

Dix felt bad for the horses. They were going on sheer training and trust, with their eyes closed to slits and their ears pinned back. If they'd had their way, they would have huddled together, rumps into the blast, and waited it out instead of trudging blindly over unfamiliar ground.

But it couldn't be helped. Dix knew where he was going, all right, if he could just see to get there. They had left the canyon behind, crossed a flat plain, and were presently following a dry riverbed. He hoped they were, anyhow. He couldn't see for beans in this howl.

But at least the wind kept Yancy's mouth closed.

Yancy was turning into a pretty fair lawman, but he could get to yammering. And yammering. And yammering. Dix supposed that most of the time he didn't mind it so much as he pretended. Leastwise, the talk filled up the air and pushed the old ghosts aside for a little while.

Odd how they still haunted him after all these years. Ramona's spirit clung to him like the odor of burnt coffee grounds, permeated his being, dug tiny hooks into his skin. And Clara. Poor little Clara. She would have been a grown woman by now, had children of her own. He would have been a grandfather, he supposed. He would have given anything if . . .

He gave his head a hard shake, forcing the ghosts away, letting the biting wind tatter their edges, fray their ancient shrouds.

Yancy, that's what he'd been thinking about.

Yancy Wade had come to him fresh from the plains of Kansas, filled with glamorous thoughts about California but without a nickel to his name, thanks to Joey Dundee and his gang. Yancy had signed on with the posse that chased down the men who'd robbed him, and then he'd signed on as deputy.

Dix had never thought to ask why a young man so het up about the Golden State and oceans and tall, thick grass would decide to stick around in the barren, alkali mountains that surrounded Gushing Rain. He was just happy that Yancy, who had comported himself with honor and grit, had decided to stay in town for a spell. He'd been impressed. He'd liked the boy, admired his style. Still did.

Not that he ever admitted it.

Of course, Yancy had his drawbacks. Aside from the nonstop gabbing morning, noon, and night, he was tall and, Dix supposed, good looking. At least, half the female population of Gushing Rain seemed to be moony over him. One gal or another was always dropping off a cake or a pie or a plate of cookies at the jail for Yancy. Hell, the place was more cluttered than a bake shop half the time. And just last week, Lizzie Resnell had brought him a whole platter of fried chicken!

Of course, Dix had eaten about half of that chicken himself, so he supposed he couldn't really count being handsome or sought after as one of Yancy's drawbacks. The Lord knew, nobody'd ever brought *him* a plate of food on account of his hair or his eyes or his winsome ways.

Dix was as ugly as ten miles of bad road, and he knew it. Short, too. He was barely five foot nine in his boots— five seven or thereabouts in his stocking feet—and he had to look up to everybody, including his young deputy, who was six foot two. But he'd figured out a lot of years ago that looking up to people was a lot different literally than metaphorically.

He might be a sawed-off little son of a bitch and so homely that nobody'd ever bake him a pie, but folks respected him, by God. He'd been Gushing Rain's sheriff for almost six years. He was an honorable man—or tried his best to be—and he did his job with no fuss, no muss.

The wind took another quick turn, and for a few seconds he couldn't even see Yancy and Cash riding beside him. He cursed himself for not stringing a tether line between the two horses, and he was about to try shouting into the gale when the wind shifted again.

And then he saw it, dimly, through the dark and the wailing blow. A cluster of low adobe houses came into view, then a flicker of lamplight, leaking almost imperceptibly through the shutters and the gale.

Inwardly, he said a small prayer of thanks, more out of long habit than because he thought anybody was listening, and urged his horse toward the light. He heard Yancy holler something at him, but he couldn't make out the words. Most of what Yancy said didn't matter, anyway. It could wait.

He rode up to the front door of the adobe with the faintly lighted window—two windows, he could see now—and dismounted, hanging onto the saddle horn for dear life when a hard gust came up behind him.

Yancy hollered at him again, and this time Dix heard him. "Where in tarnation are we?" Yancy shouted.

"Regret," he shouted back. He handed his reins to Yancy, staggered to the door, and began to pound on it.

When the banging started, Nancy MacGregor dropped her ladle into the pot of pronghorn stew with a splat. Storms always put the fear of God into her, anyway, especially these big cheats of dry windstorms that thundered and lightninged and promised rain, but rarely produced it. The adobe was snug enough, but now the storm seemed to have focused on her front door. Her only door.

But a half second after the ladle splashed into the stew, she realized that the pounding was rhythmic. Not storm sound at all. The moan and screech of the wind had finally taken its toll on her, she told herself. The unrelenting wail of it would make anybody half crazy.

"Just a minute!" she cried, certain it was Enrique, come to check on her and the children, although that in itself was certainly queer. But who else could it be? Enrique's wife, Soledad, would never venture out in this wind, and old Julio was likely tucked up in the barn with his goats and his mescal.

She quickly covered the stew with a cast-iron lid and snugly covered the cornbread and the peach pie. Enrique had brought those tinned peaches all the way from Yuma on his last trip there, and they were like gold. It wouldn't do to have her pie blown all full of dirt and twigs, now, would it?

Bang, bang, bang, went the door. Didn't Enrique realize she had to get things nailed down before she opened it?

"Quick, the plates!" she said to James, who was already gathering them as fast as a scurrying beetle. He slid them back into the cupboard.

"Get back and cover your faces," she warned the children as she stepped to the door.

James was ahead of her once more. He had pulled Melody out of the way and was leading her into the shadows on the far side of the fireplace. Nancy counted to three, stepped to the side, and yanked up the latch.

She yelped in surprise, couldn't help it, when the door blew back on its hinges. It slammed the inside wall and let in a hard gust of dirt and grit and growing things the storm had picked up miles away.

She would have stern words with Enrique, coming over here in a blow. What nerve! Maybe Soledad had thrown him out again, but couldn't he have gone to the barn instead, where he could have drowned his misery in Julio's mescal? Now she'd have to clean the whole front room from top to bottom all over again!

But the man who stepped through the door—was blown through it, more like—wasn't Enrique.

Her hands came up to her mouth in terror at the first sight of him, for his bandanna was pulled up over his nose and mouth in the manner of a highwayman, and he was caked black with dirt and grime. The wildness of the storm whirled around him. But then she saw something glinting dully on his chest, beneath the covering of dust, that made her relax. The silver of a badge.

He looked at her and blinked twice in what she took to be surprise.

But if he had been shocked to find a white woman here,

he recovered quickly. "Sorry to intrude, ma'am," he shouted over the wind. "There's three of us. We'd appreciate—"

"Come in, come in!" she shouted back at him. This country, this land! Where else would two people have to shout when they were only two steps from each other?

But he stayed put and yelled, "Horses!"

Blast, she should have thought of that! She answered, "Barn!" and pointed out into the blackness, then added, "Come back, Marshal, I'll feed you!"

He gave a terse tug to his hat brim, then hauled the door back from the wall and, with some struggle, closed it after him. He took the worst of the wind away with him, but the house was in ruins, at least to Nancy's mind. There was a bucket's worth of storm debris strewn against the far wall, dust hung thick in the air, and the table and chairs were covered in settling grit.

Well, no sense in cleaning it up just yet. He'd bring half the territory in with him when he came back.

She shook out her apron, and while the dust from it was still rising, she said, "All right, children."

James, tow-headed and blue-eyed and so serious and grim that it made her heart ache, peeked out from around the corner of the fireplace with ancient eyes. Poor, strange little James. So old to be only eleven.

"It's a marshal," she said, smiling reassuringly. "Caught out in the storm. I believe he has two friends with him. I've invited them to eat with us."

James came out then, dully tugging his younger sister behind him, and cutting a wide berth around the fireplace. So heartbreakingly odd, these children, so lost.

Nancy would have been hard-pressed to say which was the more wounded of the two. James had come to her wild-eyed and full of rage, and missing the last two fingers on his left hand. He still hadn't told her how he'd lost them, though it had been nearly a year since the lone Apache had come. The Indian had ridden as close as the far side of the dry riverbed and tossed James and his sister down like two dead rabbits before he wheeled his pony and took off.

They scarcely weighed more than rabbits, as it turned out. They were knobby-kneed and sunken of belly and showed every rib, but they took to regular meals with a vengeance and soon gained weight. Despite feeding them and loving them the best she knew how, James's eyes were alternately sullen and full of distrust, or so angry that it frightened her.

And then there was Melody. Nine years old and as blond-headed and blue-eyed as her brother, Nancy had at first assumed the girl was a deaf mute. It had been nearly two months before Melody had jumped at a sound— Soledad had dropped a bucket—and Nancy realized that she could hear. But she might as well be deaf, since she still paid scant attention to anything or anyone around her and had yet to utter a single word. James did all the talking for both of them, although that was precious little.

James was staring at her. Melody stared at the dirt floor.

"Perhaps the marshal will have stories to tell," she offered in an enthusiastic tone. There was no response. She had learned not to expect any, although that didn't keep her from trying.

She made another stab at it. "Would you like a glass of limeade while we wait for our guests?"

The wind gusted down the chimney, momentarily pushing flames and ash out over the hearth and rattling the covered stew pot resting there.

James's eyes flicked to it, then back to her. "No," he said, and helped his little sister to a chair.

· · ·

"A white woman, you say?" Yancy shouted for the third time.

They had found the barn, which was inhabited by a flock of milling goats, perhaps a dozen roosting chickens, a dusty and disused buckboard wagon, and one very old— and very inebriated—Mexican. When they'd first come banging in, the wind blowing a storm of hay and straw across the floor and spooking the goats, the old man had tried to stagger to his feet with little success. He sat down hard on his bed of straw and passed out before Dix and Yancy had pushed the rattling door closed behind them. How anybody could sleep with all this wind noise and all this goat stench was beyond Dix.

"Yeah, and quit askin'," Dix snapped. He reached for his saddlebags. That she had been a redheaded woman and pretty to boot was his secret, and would be until they gained the house again. He was old and he was ugly, but he could still admire a pretty woman, couldn't he? Her house had smelled like good, meaty stew and peach pie and cornbread.

What the devil was she doing in Regret?

He hadn't been down this way for several years, and at that time the town—having gone through a two-year silver boom which had long since played out—had dwindled to about a dozen souls, all Mexicans, all hard-scrabble farmers. The river was dry, but there was water underground if a man was willing to dig for it and carry it to the crops.

But it looked to him like the population had sunk to practically nothing. At least, while they'd fought their way to the barn—which in better times had been the town livery—he'd seen only one other little house with signs of life. What was a nice redheaded lady doing in a place like this?

He supposed he'd be finding out shortly.

With a sigh, he slung his saddlebags over his shoulder, then picked up his and Yancy's rifles, kneeing a nanny goat out of his way in the process.

There were three stalls remaining in the barn, the rest having been cleared out to make room for the goats, he supposed. Any shelter was a godsend in a blow like this (even if it did reek of goats) and the barn itself was adobe, with walls three feet thick. It wasn't going anywhere, even if its big coach doors threatened to take off for parts unknown at any given moment.

And three stalls was a wealth when you only had two horses. Their board and pole walls would keep the billy goat at bay, anyhow. The goat lowered its horns off and on in a vague threat and intermittently pawed the ground, its bell clanging, but so far it hadn't charged.

"Was she pretty?" asked Cash. Yancy had cuffed him to a tether ring before they tended the horses, and was in the process of uncuffing him.

They were all yelling to be heard over the wind, but the old Mexican snored through it all. Dix was sorely tempted to see if there was any Who Hit John left in the old geezer's jug. He could have done with a belt, he was that used up.

"Not your type, Cash," Yancy said.

"How do you know, Deputy Wade?" Cash replied testily. "You didn't even see her!"

"Don't need to see her to figure she's not the type to want to set up housekeepin' in jail." Yancy clamped the empty cuff around Cash's other wrist and closed it with a click.

"Aw, Jeez!" said Cash in dismay. "I was just askin'!"

Dix waited while they crossed the barn's floor and joined him. He put a hand on the rattling door's latch. It vibrated under his hand. "Ready?" he shouted, mentally girding himself for the coming onslaught.

"Can't we just stay in here?" wailed Cash, whose hat had blown off somewhere along the way.

"Will you shut up?" shouted Yancy.

"Shoe's on the other foot, ain't it?" Dix muttered a little smugly and, motioning them to the side, let the wind take the door.

3

It was a very strange group that gathered at Nancy Mac-Gregor's table that evening.

Three men—the oldest one shortish and dark, and his deputy, very tall and very blond, and their prisoner, sandy-haired, young enough to be her son, and whose height was right in the middle of the other two—sat like stair steps along one side of her table.

Introductions had been made all around. She had offered water and soap and towels, and they'd scrubbed the worst of the grime from their hands and faces, but she would have felt better if they'd each had a good dunking in the horse trough out in front of the barn.

They'd "ma'am'd" her to death in the past fifteen minutes. She hadn't been called ma'am so much in years, not since . . . Well, not since before. It made her feel strangely melancholy, as if she should have some pretty needlework to put aside, then summon Ewan from the fields or the back room to meet their guests. But he would not come. He would never come again.

The children sat across from the men. Melody silently

eyed her plate, waiting for someone to ladle food onto it. James eyed the marshal. No, she corrected herself, the sheriff. He'd told her: "Sheriff Dix Granger from up north at Gushing Rain, ma'am." The tall young man with the other badge pinned to his chest was his deputy, Yancy Wade. And the boy who was presently hiding his cuffed hands in his lap was Cash Malone. Whatever had he done? He certainly seemed a nice enough lad.

"Sure smells good, ma'am," Deputy Wade said as he unlocked Cash's handcuffs and slid him a warning look.

She already had the deputy marked as a good eater. He watched her bringing the stewpot, and he was the next thing to drooling. And it was all he could do, she noticed, to keep his hands off the cornbread and honey that were already on the table.

"I hope you'll enjoy it," she said as she set it down. She lifted the lid, and fragrant steam rose.

"Plates?" she said, and began to ladle it out.

It was a good thing that Enrique had shot the antelope that morning, and that she'd made a big enough pot to feed the children and herself for the next several days. She had a feeling that their usual fare would be just enough for one of these men to inhale.

As it was, Deputy Wade had his plate cleaned by the time she finished filling the last one, and he said, "Is there seconds, ma'am?" before she had a chance to sit down.

"Nancy?" said James. He was still sitting at his untouched plate with folded hands, and he was glaring at Deputy Wade.

"It's all right for tonight, James," she said quietly. "You can go ahead." She took Deputy Wade's plate and filled it again, but when she handed it back to him, Sheriff Granger reached across Cash Malone to grab the deputy's fork hand.

"You'll have to pardon those of us who haven't got any manners," he said. He hadn't touched his food yet. He shot his deputy a stern look, then added, "Ma'am, I'd be honored if you'd say grace."

Deputy Wade colored a little, shook his hand free, and said, "Beg pardon, ma'am. Guess I forgot myself in the face of all these good eats."

"Hardy-har-har," brayed Cash Malone.

"Shut up, or you'll be eating outside in the blow," Sheriff Granger snapped under his breath. She heard him, though, and bit her lip to hold back the smile. He bowed his head, and the other men—and James—followed suit.

Nancy stared for a moment at the four bowed heads—and little Melody's, blankly staring—before she, too, lowered her head and said, "Heavenly Father, we thank You for this bounty of which we are about to partake. We also thank You for shepherding these men out of the storm and bringing them safely to our table. Amen."

The men softly echoed her "amen" and immediately pounced with gusto upon their plates.

She smiled.

Dix had a lot of questions. He hadn't seen another horse in the barn. How the hell did she manage? How did she get out for supplies?

And where had these children come from? The little girl hadn't spoken a word, but the little boy, who was clearly the girl's brother, and who was missing two fingers, called the MacGregor woman by her given name. These weren't her kids. He was certain of that. They'd been Indian captives, if he didn't miss his guess. He'd seen the boy's wary look before.

But why would the Army settle reclaimed children with

someone who lived as far out as Regret? *Remote* didn't begin to describe it by half.

It took him all through supper and halfway through his peach pie before he figured out where to start.

"Storm's quieted down some," he said, just to get the conversation started. Everybody had been pretty intent on their plates. It was toothsome stew, and the cornbread was sweet and tender.

"Yes, it has quieted," she said, and smiled pleasantly.

Yancy helped himself to a second slice of pie. It was plumb embarrassing, the way that boy ate. Yancy said, "You never can tell with these howlers, ma'am. They can come and go in an hour or rip up the scrub all night long. Why, one time, I remember as how—"

"Hadn't you best feed that tapeworm, Yancy?" Dix asked.

Yancy shrugged and dug into his pie.

"I saw lights in another adobe, Mrs. MacGregor," Dix continued. She certainly was a handsome looking woman! A fine figure, auburn hair with a touch of silver threaded through, and large, clear blue eyes. She had a widow's peak that made her face appear heart-shaped. He liked that. She was a little shorter than he was. He supposed, if he had his boots off, that they'd be of a height. What had happened to her man?

"That would be the Valdezes," she replied, her hands folded on the table. It was crudely built of planks, but she had it waxed to a sheen. "Enrique Valdez and his wife, Soledad. I suppose you met Julio when you were in the barn?"

Cash Malone, uncuffed for the meal, snorted. "Not hardly. He was passed out drunk."

Between bites, Yancy elbowed him and said, "Shut up, thief."

"Sorry," Cash replied snidely. "Keep forgettin' I'm the prisoner around here, on account of you never remind me."

Dix ignored them. To Mrs. MacGregor he said, "How many others in town?"

She shrugged. "That's all there are, anymore, I'm afraid. Actually, it's a good thing that you came when you did. Not that I would have wished this storm on anybody, you understand. But poor old Samuel died about a month ago, and now we have no way to bring supplies in."

She paused to take a sip of her coffee, and Dix and Yancy, almost at the same time, said, "Sorry, ma'am."

Dix added, "My condolences."

To his surprise, she laughed. "Oh, dear! Samuel was our mule! I'm sorry if you thought otherwise."

Yancy blushed, and Dix smiled sheepishly. Cash muttered, "Glad somebody told me to shut up," and forked his mouth full of peach pie.

"Would it be possible for you gentlemen to carry Enrique to a town where he could buy another mule or a horse?" she asked. "I wouldn't ask, but it's quite a ride to civilization. I don't like to contemplate how long it would take on foot. Enrique isn't as young as he once was. And now that these windstorms have settled in to plague us again . . ."

"Be happy to, ma'am," Yancy offered.

Dix shook his head. "Whoa up, Yancy. What he means to say, Mrs. MacGregor, is that we'd be pleased to send somebody back for this Enrique, or maybe bring a horse out to him. We're sort of overloaded on this trip. Only got two mounts between the three of us."

" 'Cause some damned fool galloped his nag square into a badger hole," Yancy added under his breath.

"Quit it!" said Cash, suddenly angry. "It's bad enough I had to shoot my Dusty. You don't need to go harpin' on it. All the time we were in the barn, it was yack, yack,

yack about how it was my fault!" he said, tears in his eyes.

"Settle down, the both of you," Dix warned. He felt halfway sorry for Cash. Yancy had harped on the subject of the horse a little too much, although Dix had let him get away with it. Yancy's gelding was strong, but riding double for miles in a battering wind had strained him, and Yancy had taken it out on Cash.

"I loved poor old Dusty," Cash was saying. Glumly, he stared at his pillaged plate. "Daddy'd had him since he was a yearling."

"Can we go to bed, Nancy?" said a small but very adult voice from across the table. The boy. James, that was his name. Poor kid. How had he lost those fingers?

"Certainly," she said, although she didn't look the least bit surprised.

This struck Dix as odd. He'd checked his watch earlier, and it couldn't be much more than seven now, seven-thirty at the latest. If he'd been her, he would have been over there feeling that boy's forehead. Nobody's kids asked to go to bed early! What would they ask for next, a dose of castor oil?

But then, maybe he'd been too long removed from the company of children. He sat and watched as the boy rose from his chair, carried his and his sister's plates to the washbasin, then took her hand and headed for a small, arched doorway at the back of the room.

"I'll come to tuck you up in a few minutes," Nancy MacGregor said. The children gave no sign that they'd heard her, just scuffed through the door.

Brightly, as if it were normal for children to never break a smile, to stack their plates without being asked, and to volunteer for bed, Mrs. MacGregor turned toward him again and said, "More coffee, Sheriff Granger?"

"Right nice of you," he said.

The wind rattled the door and shutters again. The storm, which had momentarily lulled, was gathering itself for a new assault. As she topped off his cup, he said, "Looks like we're in for another pounding."

"You're well out of it," she replied, and she was just turning to fill Cash's outstretched cup when they heard the shot.

"That what I think it was?" asked Yancy.

Dix was already on his feet. He grabbed his hat. "That old man in the barn fond of shooting things up when he's sozzled, ma'am?" He picked up his rifle.

"Oh, Lord," breathed Mrs. MacGregor. She wasn't listening, just staring forlornly at the front door, one hand still holding the coffeepot, the other hand pressed over her heart. "She's finally shot him."

"Who?" yelled Yancy. He had his rifle, too, and was already at the door, his hand on the latch. "Who shot who?"

Dix joined Yancy. "You coming?" he asked Cash.

"Or maybe he's shot her," said Mrs. MacGregor, to no one in particular.

Still seated at the table, Cash nonchalantly reached over and snagged the next to the last piece of pie. "Don't look at me," he said, shrugging and wide-eyed, playing innocent. "I'm the prisoner, remember?"

Dix lifted his bandanna over his nose. "Go," he said to Yancy.

The two of them pushed out into the storm.

Yancy lost Dix in the first thirty seconds. The blow had come up fast, worse than before, and he couldn't tell if there was a moon tonight or if the storm clouds had erased it from view. All Yancy knew for sure was that he couldn't see a blessed thing. He'd been stumbling around for about five minutes when he found the Mexican woman. He practically tripped over her, in fact.

She was on her knees in the dirt, the wind whipping her skirts and shawl, the wild gale concealing her until he was nearly on top of her. And the first thing she did was whirl and point a rifle up into his belly.

"Jesus!" he yelped, and tried to jump back. The wind pushed him forward again. "Don't shoot!" he cried, staggering to keep his balance.

"I kill!" she shouted. "I see and I kill! Why has the wind come to torment me? The devils! These devils will not have me for their fire!"

Yancy didn't know what the hell to say to her. What did you say to crazy people, anyway, especially crazy women? Crazy Mexican women! He was about to try something, though, maybe tell her that he was the law, or tell her it wasn't nice to go around shooting people you didn't know in the stomach, or that maybe they should talk about this someplace out of the wind.

But then a man—not Dix, as he'd hoped, but a Mexican—fought his way into view. He came up on the other side of the woman and wrested the rifle from her hands.

She didn't give him much of a fight. In fact, she grabbed his knee and hung on for dear life.

"Soledad!" the stranger shouted. "What have you done?"

"He will not burn me, Enrique!" she shouted. "We will not burn! I have seen to that!"

Just then, Enrique seemed to notice Yancy. He swung the rifle up again and shouted, "Who are you? What do you want here?"

Yancy only wanted another piece of pie and a quiet place to eat it, but here he was, leaning back into a raging wind again, and at gunpoint, to boot. But at least this man appeared lucid. It was more than he could say for the woman.

He pointed to his badge. "Law!" he shouted. "I'm the law!"

The man wiggled the rifle at him. *"¿Que?"* he shouted back. *"¿Que?"*

And then, out of the roiling gale, came Dix. He just appeared out of nowhere like he'd been launched from a catapult, and he flew right over the crazy woman. He hit the man from the side, and the two of them toppled back into the storm and disappeared.

Yancy tried to move, but the woman had latched herself to his leg. She was laughing now, shouting, "No burn, no burn! I kill him! I kill them all!"

He tried to break free but succeeded only in tripping himself. As he fell forward onto his face, he heard the rifle discharge again and felt a familiar burning in his arm and his side.

"Shit!" he yelped, and felt tears flood his eyes. Despite the searing pain, he tried to free his own rifle from beneath his body, to bring it up.

But the crazy woman was crawling up his body now, crawling fast, clawing her way up his leg to his hip, his waist. He kicked at her, seeking to free himself so that he could turn over and find someone to shoot at—hopefully, the person who'd shot at him—through the pelting wind and the darkness.

"Dix?" he yelled into the howling blackness. "Dix!" He kicked at the woman again. "Get off'a me, you mad cat!"

He gave up on the rifle and reached for his holster. He freed the Peacemaker just as the woman clambered onto his back.

"Off, goddamn it!" he shouted, taking in a mouthful of grit for his trouble. He rolled over, hard, onto his hurt left arm and side.

Yancy nearly cried out from the pain, but it got the woman off him. He pushed her away, pushed himself up to his knees, and blindly aimed the pistol into the roil.

"Dix!" he shouted again. "Dix!"

4

Dix came up on Yancy's right, saw the pistol in his hand, and clamped a hand on his shoulder.

Yancy spun around toward him. For a half second, Dix was afraid his own deputy was going to shoot him, but a gust of wind took Yancy over on his side before he could get a shot off.

"It's me, you blamed fool," Dix shouted, then braced himself and put a hand down.

While he struggled to help Yancy stand up, the man he'd bulldogged was leaning into the wind, assisting the woman to her feet. When he gestured for them to follow him to Mrs. MacGregor's little house, they gave him no argument.

Although it seemed to Dix that they lost ground with every step, the four of them, heads bowed into the wind, gained the adobe at last. The gale spat them through the door, and once they'd closed it, they collapsed where they stood, panting, exhausted, their mouths and noses clogged with dust.

Yancy spoke first. He'd lost his hat, and he held his

head down. Grit slowly sifting from his hair, he coughed, then said, "The Lord must have it in for us. I never seen it blow so bad."

He might have had more to say, but he commenced coughing again.

Dix was doubled over, his hands on his knees. His mouth gritted. He still had his hat, but he felt like he'd inhaled half the territory, and his already sore muscles ached from fighting the wind again. He was too old for these storms, he thought, too old to be sheriffing, too old for Arizona. And especially, too old for what was coming next.

"Oh, you poor laddie!" Dix heard Mrs. MacGregor cry. He looked up just in time to see her lead Yancy to a chair next to Cash. Was that blood on Yancy's arm? Great, just great. The last thing he needed right now was a wounded deputy.

Despite his complaining back, he forced himself to stand up. He had business to attend to.

On his left, against the wall, leaned the panting Mexican couple. Gray with dust, the woman was on her knees and clinging to the man's leg. He had bent to put an arm around her quaking shoulders and was mumbling soothing words in her ear.

"Soledad and Esteban Valdez?" he asked hoarsely.

"I am Enrique," corrected the man. He didn't look over. All his attention was on his wife. "Why are you here?"

"We were out after a thief," Dix said. He could have used a long drink of water, but he'd ask for it later. He pointed toward the table and Cash Malone. "Out after him. That you shootin' out there?"

"It was my Soledad," Enrique answered.

At last he turned toward Dix. He was a pleasant enough looking man—or at least, Dix supposed he was, beneath the grit. He was middle-aged, clean shaven, trim from long hours in the field, and of moderate height, maybe a tad shorter than Dix was.

"When the storm quiets, she takes the rifle," Enrique explained. "She is gone before I know it."

"I heard him out there, Enrique," Soledad said. Her tone was one of satisfaction. Dix had yet to see her face, which was covered with a shawl. "I heard him. I will always hear them, I will always smell their stench. They cannot hide from me."

Enrique stroked her shoulder. "*Sí,* Soledad," he said, but he looked at Dix and shrugged sadly.

"Well, what in the holy heck happened out there?" piped up Cash. "Who fired those shots?"

Dix ignored him. He went to Enrique, helped him lift Soledad to her feet, and walked her to the table. She was quite tiny; slender and barely five feet tall. As she sat down, her shawl fell away from her grit-caked face to puddle about her shoulders. Her profile was delicate, and her lips were full and sensuous, but when she turned toward him, it was all he could do not to visibly shrink back.

Cash had no such reticence. "Jesus H. Christ, lady!" he yelped before he remembered himself. "I mean . . . sorry."

She had snatched up her shawl again by that time, but Dix had seen. They all had. The left side of her face was hideously scarred from long-ago burns. The eye was dead and milky white, and the flesh around it, and that of the cheek, was contorted and cruelly drawn with scar tissue.

Behind her, Enrique stood, his hands protectively on her shoulders. "Apache," he mouthed soundlessly at Dix, as if that one word could explain it all. Actually, it did.

"You children get back to bed," he heard Mrs. MacGregor say, and he looked just in time to see the nightshirted boy and girl turn and scuff back through the doorway.

She had pulled down a little basket of medicines from someplace and, carefully, she washed the grime from

Yancy's forearm. "The bullet passed through cleanly, Sheriff," she said to Dix, "and it didn't hit the bone. Then it nicked his side, but just barely. No digging." She set aside her washcloth, gently patted his arm dry with a clean towel, then picked up a little tin of salve. "He'll be all right."

"That's easy enough for you to say, ma'am," Yancy muttered. He flinched when she began to apply the medicine.

Dix helped himself to the water and swallowed most of the grit in his teeth. If this kept up, he'd have a gizzard full of gravel, like a bird.

"Julio all right?" Enrique asked. He had pulled out a handkerchief, and he blew his nose with a long honk. "She did not shoot him? Sometimes . . . sometimes she thinks . . ." He stared down at his wife.

"Don't know for sure about Julio," Dix said, drawing a hand over his face. The shutters were banging. Didn't this wind ever stop? "I didn't check on him. But I believe we accounted for those two shots."

"I only took one slug, Dix," Yancy said. He was studying Mrs. MacGregor, who was swathing his forearm in bandages. "Who the hell shot me, anyhow?"

"The gun, it just went off when the sheriff and I were on the ground," said Enrique, somewhat sheepishly. "Many apologies, Deputy."

Yancy nodded in acceptance, but he grumbled, "You could'a shot me clean through the head, mister! In the future, don't go waving rifles around when you can't see what you're aimin' at, all right?" And then he turned his attention to a new sphere. "Hey, any of that pie left?"

There was one piece, and Yancy leaned forward and scooped it up in his hand before Cash could grab it. "Well, I'm injured," he muttered defensively around the first big bite. "A shot-up man needs his nourishment."

No one paid much attention, though. Cash and Mrs. MacGregor, her hands full of bandages, were both staring curiously at Dix. She said, "Both shots were accounted for? Please tell me it wasn't one of our goats!"

Soledad lifted her head and cackled, "No goat!"

"No goat," Dix echoed grimly. "A man. I found him over by the barn, where the wind rolled him."

Mrs. MacGregor blanched, but both Cash and Yancy leaned toward him. Yancy, the half-eaten pie in his hand and paused inches from his mouth, said, "Dix? She shot a fella?"

Mrs. MacGregor said, "But there's no one else here besides Julio!"

"There is now," Dix said wearily. "Or there was. Believe you had an uninvited guest, ma'am."

"We will not burn," said Soledad happily. "I have seen to it."

Dix wanted to slap her, but he ignored her instead. He said, "Soledad shot an Apache brave. He's dead. I checked. Reckon he got caught out in the storm and was looking for cover. The land's flat as a griddle for miles around here. This is the only place where a man can get out of the wind halfway decent."

Soledad began to laugh. It made the hair on the back of Dix's neck stand on end.

"Enrique?" Dix asked through clenched teeth. "Can you do something about her?"

Mrs. MacGregor tipped her head toward the doorway and said, "My bed," and Enrique guided Soledad, tittering, from the front room.

That left Cash, Yancy, Mrs. MacGregor, and Dix to stare at each other.

"The poor thing's the same as killed us, hasn't she?" Nancy MacGregor said, as matter-of-factly as if she were announcing that morning had come or that the sky was blue.

She'd sized up the situation, all right. Dix didn't know why that brave had been out here—either scouting or hunting, most like—but there were apt to be at least one or two others with him. Maybe more. That they'd been separated in the storm was a given. If there'd been more than the one, there'd have been Apaches on the roof and down the chimney by now. But come morning, somebody'd be scouting for him. Somebody who'd be plenty ticked off once they found out their pal was dead. They'd be looking for blood.

With only two horses, they couldn't make a run for it. And with only five men to stand them off—one injured, one barely growing whiskers, and one passed out drunk in the barn—he didn't figure the odds to be in their favor.

"Aw, shit!" Cash said. He dug into his pockets, pulled out the fifty dollars he'd stolen from Old Man Peterson's bank, and threw it on the table in a shower of wadded paper and jangling coins. "I'm gonna take my chances in the storm."

He was halfway out of his chair when Dix pulled him back down. "Nobody's going anywhere. At least not right now. And I apologize for his language, ma'am."

Yancy looked at him leerily. "Dix?"

"That's not fair!" Cash railed. "I'm not even supposed to be here!"

"Tough," Dix said. He was inclined to say that he wasn't supposed to be here, either. If it hadn't been for Cash and that fool stunt he'd pulled at the bank, he would have been back in Gushing Rain. He would have been sipping coffee and eating Yancy's baked goods and sorting wanted posters at this very minute.

But all he said was, "Well, you're here now. If you go out in that blow, you're liable to walk smack into one of those braves. That is, if the wind doesn't blow you to Mexico first." To Mrs. MacGregor, he asked, "Can Yancy ride?"

"There'll be pain," she answered quizzically, "but he can manage."

"Whoa up a minute!" said Yancy. "Dix, if you're thinkin' what I think you're thinkin', you can just—"

"Give it a rest, Yancy," he said firmly.

"What?" Cash cut in angrily. "What's he thinkin'? Has everybody gone loco? We've all gotta get out of here, and now! You got any idea of what Apaches do to folks they take a dislike to?"

Dix saw a look pass over Nancy MacGregor's face, just a shadow, faint and fast, but it lingered long enough to tell him that she knew, all right. That she had known an Apache's anger personally, and not just from whatever had happened to those poor kids in the back room. And by the look on her face, that Apache's anger had been horrible indeed.

"Shut up, Cash," he warned.

Nancy MacGregor wasn't just talking earlier. She had already decided they were dead.

She might just be right.

Cash shouted, "I got just as much say in this as anybody!" He pounded the table with his fists so hard that the dishes rattled and the coins jumped. "I want out, and I want out right now! You hear me, Sheriff Granger?"

Dix didn't even think. In one motion, he turned, brought up his fist, and slugged Cash hard in the jaw. There was a satisfying pop, and Cash fell over backward. He took the chair with him and landed with a crash, dazed and blinking.

Quickly, Dix pulled the cuffs from his pocket and secured the boy's wrist to the table leg. As he clicked the lock closed, he muttered, "Told you to shut up. You'd best listen to me, boy."

When he sat down again, Nancy MacGregor and Yancy

were staring at him. "You'll have to excuse Cash, ma'am," he said curtly. "He's had hard times lately."

"Man," muttered Yancy, staring down at Cash. "I'll bet that hurt."

Dix said, "This wind's gonna die down well before the dawn, but there's no moon but a sliver. You can't travel till light."

Yancy opened his mouth long enough to get out, "Dix!" But the sheriff silenced him with a wave of his hand.

"Somebody's got to go for help," he said, and his voice was just as serious as he could make it. "I don't trust Cash. The old man in the barn's a drunk, and Enrique's got his hands full with that crazy woman. It's you, Yancy."

But Yancy crossed his arms over his chest and said, "No. You'll need me here, you stubborn old mule! It's my left arm that's banged up, Dix! I can still shoot with my right!"

Dix nodded. "I know. And whoever I send back to Gushing Rain may have to do a little shooting along the way. We don't know where those other Apaches are."

Yancy remained silent, but the muscles in his jaw were working overtime.

"Take my Dasher," Dix went on. "That Chunk horse of yours is a good sprinter, but Dasher'll be faster over the long haul. If you leave at first light and go like the devil's after you, you can be back with help in two days. That's an order, Deputy."

After a moment's grim hesitation, Yancy said, "Yessir."

Enrique emerged from the back of the house just then. He eyed Cash, who was still on the floor and holding his head, but he didn't comment. Instead, he simply said, "She is asleep."

While Nancy MacGregor cleared the table and did the dishes, the men sat silently at the table, listening to the shutters rattle and the wind howl.

• • •

Later, when Nancy went to check on the children, she
found James still awake. She set the lamp on his little bed-
side table, then perched on the edge of the mattress.

She would have touched him, smoothed his brow, but
she knew that he'd only cringe away, then turn his head as
if her touch was a fire under which he was bravely bear-
ing up.

So she folded her hands in her lap and said, "Were you
listening?"

He nodded, just once. "They're coming."

"Yes," she said. "I'm afraid they are." She would have
given anything if this child would have suffered a hug, if
he would have thrown his arms about her.

Or cried.

Or gotten angry.

Anything.

But without expression, he said, "Tomorrow," and
closed his eyes.

5

By roughly two in the morning, the storm closed up shop for the night. Dix, who had been dozing off and on, rose and stepped across Yancy's snoring form to nudge Cash with his boot. That was all it took to wake the boy. Cash sat up on the floor, wide-eyed and ready, like he was expecting Satan's minions at any second. Dix figured the boy was likely right about that.

"Come on," he whispered, bending down to remove Cash's handcuffs. "Get up. We've got work to do."

"Take your deputy," the boy hissed angrily, rubbing at his wrists. "Look at that! They left a red mark!"

Dix grabbed his collar and hauled him to his feet. Quietly, but with stern purpose, he said, "Move, you little peckerwood."

"All right, all right!" whispered Cash as he slouched toward the door.

A few minutes later, they were outside in the crisp, moonless night and had made their way to the barn by the glow from Dix's lantern. These cool, clear aftermaths were the single good thing about duststorms, so far as Dix was concerned. Here it was, halfway through August, and he almost needed a jacket!

"Why've *I* gotta drag him?" Cash asked sourly.

Dix was holding the lantern above the Apache's body. He also carried two shovels, which he'd just retrieved from the barn, where the aging Mexican still snored and a dozen or so goats dozed.

Dix was thinking that Soledad might be as crazy as a bronc in the locoweed, but she was sure a keen hand with a rifle. She'd shot the Apache right through the heart. Probably killed him instantly.

The brave couldn't have been more than twenty. He was dressed in typical Apache garb, with what looked like a hammered silver dollar suspended around his neck and a woman's bracelet around his wrist. Dix didn't want to think where that bracelet had come from.

The Apache's body was a tad banged up around the edges, though, due to the storm. The wind had rolled him a good ways, then slammed him up against the adobe of the barn, face first. His nose was smashed in, and half his face was pulp.

"I don't want to touch him!" Cash was saying. "He's probably crawlin' with Apache bugs an' vermin!"

"His lice aren't no different than yours," Dix said. "Grab his feet."

They started down the side of the barn, Cash dragging the corpse by his soft leather boots and Dix following with the shovels and the lantern. "Pardon me all to hell for sayin' it," Cash puffed in obvious disgust, "but you're crazier'n a loon. Can't figure why anybody'd want to bury an Apache. If we're gonna do anything with him, we should just haul him out into the desert and let the coyotes and buzzards have him. It's what the damn savages do with their own."

"That what you heard, is it?"

"Yeah."

"Well, it's a little more complicated than that," Dix said without further explanation. He doubted Cash would have much sympathy with—or interest in—actual Apache burial customs. "And you can stop here."

Unceremoniously, Cash let the dead brave's legs drop. They were at the rear of the barn now, next to the manure pile. Dix set down the lantern, tossed a shovel to Cash, and drove his into the hard soil.

"Dig," he said. "And don't go thinkin' you could bash my skull in with that shovel. I got eyes in the back of my head, boy."

Cash grunted. "Here I ain't even sentenced yet, and you're already metin' out cruel and unusual punishment." But he dug, just the same.

Whether Cash voiced it or not, Dix knew that he was as anxious to hide the body as anyone. There was a slim chance—a very slim one—that if those braves came looking for their companion and failed to turn him up, maybe, just maybe, they'd ride on out and leave them be.

Dix tried to remain optimistic. He told himself that the Apache's pony had likely shied off and wandered for miles. The storm would have erased any track it left. His friends might not even come scouting for him this far out.

But then they were bound to, weren't they? They might find the pony, but they sure as hell wouldn't find a rider. And Dix had no intention of letting them find this man, this child, this brave with a white man's bullet through his heart.

Soledad might as well have pinned a sign to the brave's chest. A big sign that said, "We're here, come kill us."

The two men labored for over an hour, during which time they managed to make a dent barely three feet deep and a scant six feet long in the rock-hard dirt. Despite the cool night, they were both drenched in sweat.

Dix sat down where he stood. "All right," he said, mopping his face. "Stop."

Cash, who was down in the hole, wearily hopped up to sit on its rim. "Crikey," he said, and ran a sleeve over his brow. "I'll never figure grave-diggin' for a slacker's job again."

"Amen to that," said Dix.

"Well, we finally agree on somethin'."

"How come you did it, son?"

Cash turned his head, sweat dripping from his nose and hair matted crosswise to his forehead. He peered at Dix. "What? Why I robbed the bank, you mean?"

Dix just stared at him, waiting.

After a moment, Cash looked away. "None'a your dang business," he muttered.

Dix sighed. If he had been asked just the week before which of the town's young people would be the least likely to get themselves into trouble, he would have put Cash Malone at the top of the list. He supposed he was just getting old. There must have been some sign, some character flaw he'd missed. It was a rotten shame.

"Let's put him down there and get him covered," Dix said, and climbed wearily to his feet.

Dawn came too soon to suit Dix.

Soledad and the children were still inside, presumably sleeping, but Mrs. MacGregor was up with the sun. She'd found Yancy's hat, impaled on a cactus, and while she pulled the spines out with a rusty pair of pliers, Dix tacked up Dasher.

Dasher was a good horse, breedy in the head and a deep, burnished bay, with two white socks behind and a snip on his nose. He was a little too leggy to be a good cow pony, but just right for chasing down those that needed to be chased. Chunk, Yancy's bald-faced sorrel, nosed his hay in the next stall, watching.

"Don't you go bein' so smug," Dix said to Chunk as he gave Dasher's girth a final tug. One of the goats had wandered into the stall, and nibbled at his pant leg. He shooed it away without looking. "You could end up the main course at an Apache barbecue if we don't pull this off."

A groan came from the pile of straw at the barn's rear, followed by a muffled, *"Silencio, por favor, silencio."*

The old man. Dix racked his brain. Mrs. MacGregor had said his name was Julio.

"English," Dix said. After all his years in the border country, even after having been married to Ramona, his Spanish was poor, at best. He'd tried, honestly tried, but he just never had the facility for it. Although he could pick out a word or two, he couldn't put a sentence together to save his life.

With a rustle of straw, old Julio sat up, pushing aside the goat that had been standing over him. Hands pressed to his temples, he muttered, "And who are you, *señor,* the goat police?"

He'd seen the badge, then. "Half right," Dix said and backed Dasher out of his stall.

Just then, Enrique threw the barn doors open wide, letting in a soft fan of dawn light and some much-needed fresh air. There was an exodus of goats, their bells clanging. The chickens exited next, fluttering and squawking. And during it all, Enrique and the old man engaged in a rapid-fire conversation in Spanish, very little of which Dix understood.

At last, and with great difficulty, the old man got to his feet. *"Es verdad, señor?* Soledad has killed an Apache?"

"True enough," Dix said.

He led Dasher from the barn and out into the gray morning while Enrique and the old man babbled in his wake. The goats had scattered every which way, and Yancy was walking down from the MacGregor adobe, a bundle tucked beneath his bandaged arm. He waved.

"Madre de Dios," Dix heard the old man mutter behind him. At least he knew what that meant. Ramona had said it a lot—screamed it at him, more like—every time he'd told her he'd have to be gone again for a while.

Yancy met him halfway and, grinning, pointed to his hat. "Miz MacGregor picked all the pricklers out," he said. Then he slid his parcel into a saddlebag. "Made me some good grub for the ride, too," he added, fastening the buckle. "Not that I'm gonna have a heckuva lot of time to eat it. How you doin', Dasher, old son?" He gave the gelding a pat on the neck, then swung up into the saddle.

"Keep to a lope," Dix said. "You race him, he'll wear out too fast, and you'll lose time walkin' him." He paused. "Sorry, Yancy. I guess you know how to pace a horse, all right. Just get to Gushing Rain and bring back some men. A lot of 'em."

Yancy, serious for once, said, "You can trust me, Dix."

"I know."

Dix stepped back and clapped a hand on Dasher's rump. "Hurry, boy," he whispered.

As he watched Yancy and Dasher grow smaller and smaller in the distance, he became aware of the muted sound of barking. Not just idle barking, but a real oration of serious, rip-your-leg-off-and-make-you-eat-it barks.

He turned in time to see Enrique scurry from the barn and race to his little house, shouting, "I come, Papagayo, I come!" When he reached the door, he stood to one side and pushed it open.

Dix immediately understood why he'd stepped to the side, for there burst from the adobe a mottled red flash of a medium-sized dog, a dog with what looked like only half a tail, whose barks had changed from angry to businesslike, almost happy. If Enrique hadn't moved, the damned mutt would have broken both his legs.

Dix just stood there, watching, while the dog sped up and down the old dirt street scattering russet and white and speckled hens every which way. He gathered the goats, barking furiously and nipping at their heels, until he had them bunched in the center of town. The old billy goat threatened a last-minute charge, but the dog nipped him in the nose. Bleating angrily, the goat backed off.

"Take them out, Papagayo!" called Julio, and the dog proceeded to move the goats down the dry, stone-strewn bank of the old riverbed and across it, up the far bank, and past the yellowing cornfield.

"Some dog," said Dix.

"Yes, he's quite the beastie, isn't he?"

He turned his head to find that Mrs. MacGregor had come up behind him. She was just as handsome in the early-morning light as she had been the night before. More, maybe.

Smiling, she said, "Papagayo's a wizard with the goats. We're lucky to have him. He just wandered in about two years ago, and I guess he liked us, because he stayed. Will they come soon?"

It took him a second to get his mind off her hair—impossibly red, and he saw now that it was curly—and her lips—pink and plump as rosebuds—and force himself back to business. It was just the shock of seeing her so abruptly, he supposed, and against the backdrop of this barren land. She seemed a dewy illusion, an impossible mirage. She should have been in a moist, green garden somewhere, cutting flowers.

"Sheriff?" she prodded.

"No, ma'am, they won't come for a while yet," he said stoically, hoping to hide his embarrassment. Her hair made little ringlets and fairy curls all around her face. "I reckon it'll take 'em a while to scout us out. Storm wiped out all the tracks."

She smiled again, and he wanted give himself a good kick, square in the butt. But all she said was, "What would you like us to do first?"

He cleared his throat. Had he gone daft? Thinking about a soft, cool woman when there were Apache on the way! He steeled himself and said, "First, I'd best check the lay of the land."

"I'll show you," she said.

The town had fallen in on itself. Regret had never been bigger than a gnat's behind, even in its boom days. But where there had once been offices and houses and a few stores, he found squat, ramshackle structures, creaking and swaying slightly in the dawn breeze, or piles of scattered and dusty boards held down here and there with rocks, likely to keep the wind from sailing them. Outside of the adobes and the mud-brick barn, which Mrs. MacGregor told him had been the first things built in Regret, there wasn't a single structure that he would have willingly set a foot into.

"The goats and the wind have done quite a bit of damage, I guess," she said. "And then, I suppose we have, too. Right now, we're using the general store for firewood." She pointed to a heap of boards halfway down the street. Staring at it, she added softly, "Those fools should have known better than to haul all that lumber out here. The wind goes through it like an egg beater through sponge cake."

There were two streets. The first, over which they'd entered the town, paralleled the riverbed about thirty yards back from the drop-off. The adobes and a few piles of what had once been buildings were lined down one side of it for roughly a block and a half, and looked across the dry river to the cornfield and the scavenging goats, and the distant mountains beyond. To the rear of Nancy MacGregor's house, there stood a single, sun-beaten lime tree. It seemed an odd touch of green.

Behind the adobes was a second street, perhaps a block in length and long disused. Weeds grew up in its potholes. Two more adobes, a few rickety buildings, and more scrap wood lined its edges.

She showed him the garden she and Soledad had planted where the assayer's office used to stand, and the low ledge of rock, at a distance nearly indistinguishable from the flat lay of the land, where years ago, men had tunneled into the earth and found silver.

"How's the shaft holding up, Mrs. MacGregor?" he asked as they walked toward it.

"I do wish you'd call me Nancy," she said abruptly.

He was shocked, and it was all he could do to keep walking and not stop, stock-still. He said, "Beg pardon, ma'am?"

"That, too. Just stop it. Please. If we're going to fight and possibly die together, we should at least be on a first-name basis."

"Yes'm," he said automatically, then, "Sorry. Nancy."

"Better," she said. "And I shall call you Dix. Is that short for anything?"

"Bendix," he said, and he felt heat in his neck. Hell, nobody alive knew his whole first name, and here he'd blurted it out to her.

She nodded. "Well. I'll call you Dix, then."

They reached the mouth of the old mine, and Dix pried away one of the dusty boards nailed across its entrance, then another. They fell to pieces in his hand.

He bent over, squeezed through the opening, and walked in a few feet. The overhead timbers seemed a good bit sounder than the board he'd pulled free. That made sense, he supposed. They'd been protected from the battering wind for years.

He walked back a little farther, as far as the light would permit, then turned at last and joined Nancy MacGregor outside. He dusted his hat on his thigh, then asked, "Is that the only entrance?"

She nodded.

"Good," he said. He wanted to fetch a lantern and come back to investigate further. If the shaft was in decent condition, they could get back inside it and make a stand.

They had just turned back toward town when, between the houses, he saw a man in a red-checkered shirt—a man who was supposed to be cuffed safely inside Nancy's house—running toward the barn.

"Damn it, Cash!" he swore, and took off running, leaving Nancy MacGregor behind.

6

"You bone—headed idiot," Dix muttered as he shoved Cash Malone down into a chair. "How'd you expect you'd throw a saddle on Chunk while you were wearin' handcuffs? Tryin' to make off with my deputy's horse! You beat everything, you know that?"

Nancy, who had followed the parade from the barn to the house, leaned against the crude cabinet beside the sink and looked about her. The entire population of Regret, plus Dix and young Cash, was crammed into her little front room.

The children stood beside the doorway to the short hall, holding hands. Soledad was pressed against the wall next to them. Out of habit, Nancy beckoned to James. It was best to keep as much room as possible between Soledad and the children when Soledad was having one of her spells.

"I can't help it if you cuffed me to the table leg," Cash was saying. "Jeez, Sheriff Granger, who ever heard of chainin' a man to a table leg and not expectin' him to run off?"

"Always somebody else's fault, isn't it?" Dix grumbled. He turned toward Enrique and Julio, who were waiting with their hats in their hands. "How's the roof on that barn?" he asked Julio.

Julio screwed up his face. *"¿Que?"*

"The barn roof," Dix repeated. "Is it strong enough to hold your weight?"

Julio nodded. "I fix it just this spring," he added with a note of pride in his voice.

Dix nodded. "Good. I want you to climb up there and keep watch."

Julio, eager for something to do, touched the brim of his hat and slipped away without a word.

With the children safely beside her, Nancy looked over at Soledad again. Poor thing. She still stood with her spine pressed hard against the wall, her shawl drawn over the ruined half of her face. Her expression was oddly triumphant.

Enrique glanced from his wife to the sheriff and back again. If Soledad didn't know what she'd done, he certainly did, Nancy thought. It was a miracle that they were both still alive, that one of them hadn't killed the other. It would certainly be justifiable homicide on Enrique's part if he were to someday retaliate when Soledad went through one of her lunatic phases.

The spells came more and more frequently these days, lasted longer, and were increasingly worse. Such a terrible pity. Nancy remembered when Soledad had been kind, when the madness was only a murmur in the background and easily put off to tiredness or overwork. Soledad and Enrique had nursed her back to health during the dark days, after the Apaches had killed every blessed soul in her party save herself, the dark days when she hadn't cared whether she lived or died. They'd helped her learn to walk again, to trust again.

But then the children had come. Their mere presence had started Soledad spiraling into the pit.

And now Apache were coming here, to Regret. Again, Nancy pushed away the terror and despair that had threatened to overtake her since last night.

"Enrique?" Dix said, and his voice brought her back to the present, back to this little room. "Get us a couple of lanterns. I want to take a tour of that mine shaft."

"The mine, *señor*? Is it safe?"

"That's what we're going to find out. Mrs.—Nancy?"

Her mouth crooked up into a hint of a smile. Some things remained constant, didn't they? A man tripping over his own manners, for instance. "Yes, Dix?"

"I, uh . . . You got a pistol?"

She nodded.

"Is it loaded?"

She nodded again and turned to reach high into the curtained cupboards. She brought it down and showed it to him, an old Colt Navy that had been her husband's. Enrique and Julio had told her she'd still been clinging to it when they dug her from beneath the charred wagon. She didn't remember.

"Good," Dix said with a curt nod. He poked a finger toward Cash. "If he moves, shoot him in the leg."

Cash came to attention. "Sheriff!"

"Certainly," Nancy purred, and smiled at Cash. He swallowed visibly, his Adam's apple bobbing.

Against the wall, Soledad snorted. "Why don't you just kill us all?" she muttered into the air, although everyone in the room heard her. "I have saved us from those murdering pigs, but go ahead, shoot us anyway, one by one."

Enrique set down the lantern he'd just fetched. "Soledad, hush. Have not you made enough trouble already?"

She turned toward him in a rush, like a startled and

angry animal. "You make all the trouble, Enrique! You do not care that I burn! You lie! You say, 'It is going to be all right, Soledad,' but it is not. It is never going to be all right so long as your body holds breath!"

Enrique took a step toward her, hands outstretched in benevolence, in kindly sympathy. But if he hadn't yet learned how Soledad would react, Nancy had. She, too, stepped forward, pushing the children behind her.

"Just go, Enrique," she said quietly. "You and the sheriff. Soledad and I have to fix a fine, big breakfast for you men. Don't we, Soledad? Antelope steaks, perhaps?"

Distracted, Soledad's face softened, and Enrique paused, then turned and slouched to the door, scooping up the lantern as he went. "Come, Sheriff," he said. "We get another one at my house."

Dix appeared a little confused, but he followed. Dix stopped in the doorway, though, and said softly, "You sure you're gonna be all right?"

She hefted the gun. "Right as rain." She hoped she sounded more confident than she felt.

The men gone, she turned to Soledad. Pleasantly, she asked, "Would you go to the smokehouse and cut me some steaks, dear? Nice and thin, for breakfast."

Cash leaned across the table, hissing, "You gonna give that crazy bat a *knife?*"

She ignored him. "As many as you can carve off, don't you think? These men are hungry. I'll send James to gather eggs."

Soledad stood there for a moment, and then normalcy flickered into her eyes. "Yes," she said slowly, as the light of reason grew brighter. "Yes. Pronghorn steaks would be good. Why do we call it a smokehouse, Nancy? We should call it the old Garcia house, where we hang the meat to keep the coyotes away. Even with the goat meat, we don't use it for smoking or jerking. Julio jerks goat on that piece of tin, on the roof of the old Johnson *casita.*"

Nancy smiled at her, quietly relieved. Soledad was back from that dark and horrible place she visited, that place filled with ghosts and terror and pain.

Soledad walked toward the door, and Cash shrank back from her when she paused beside his chair.

"Buenos días," she said, as if she'd just noticed him. She probably had, poor thing. She looked up at Nancy. "He is extra?"

"Two extras, Soledad," Nancy said, smiling. "Both with a powerful hunger."

"Holy cats," breathed Cash once Soledad had gone out the door. "That one's plumb peach-orchard crazy, all right!"

"And you're not?" Nancy asked, arching one brow. "Honestly! Trying to steal that horse while you were handcuffed! The sheriff was right. It certainly wasn't the brightest stunt." She bent and pushed aside the cupboard's curtain, lifting out her small egg basket. She handed it over to James. "You can fetch the eggs now," she said. And if that red-speckled hen is brooding her nest, just leave her be unless you want to get pecked again."

As always, he solemnly took the basket and said, "Yes, Nancy," without expression. His hand clasped to his sister's, he left, headed for the barn.

She and Cash were alone, and the house suddenly seemed emptier than it had for months. She slid the pistol onto the counter next to the washbasin and began pulling out pans for the steaks and the eggs and the biscuits she planned to make.

"How come you live clear out here?" Cash asked. "I mean, why don't you live near a town?"

The question deserved an answer, but she was in no

mood to give it. She said, "How do you like your eggs fried?"

"Don't matter," he replied.

She began taking out the ingredients for the biscuits, measuring them into a big green-glazed bowl with a chipped rim. Once there had been a set of them, all glazed in green, all perfect. They had been her mother's. This was the lone survivor.

"What did you do to make the sheriff come chasing after you?" she asked conversationally.

"Robbed the bank," he replied a little too proudly. "Didn't you hear?"

"Perhaps I did," she said. Where were those children with the eggs? Well, she supposed it was too soon. She slid the coffeepot off the hearth and dumped out the grounds. A fresh pot was in order. "There's a lot to keep track of lately. Is this something you do often, robbing banks?"

"No, ma'am," Cash said from behind her. "My first time."

"Doesn't seem to me that you're too good at it, my laddie," she said, rinsing out the pot. She'd best send James for a fresh bucket of water, too. This one was almost gone. "I'd look into another line of work, if I were you."

"Ma'am?"

His voice was suddenly too close. She spun around, knocking over the coffeepot, to find him standing only a foot away and pointing her own gun at her heart.

"Put that down this second!" she snapped, even though as she said it, she knew he wasn't a child she could discipline.

"No," said Cash.

She put her hands on her hips. "Don't be foolish," she said, hoping all the while that the quaking she felt inside didn't show. "If you're going to make a run for the barn again, you should know that Julio's on the roof, and Julio was a sniper in the Mexican War. He was decorated, too! He'll pick you off before you get halfway down the street."

"You'll pardon me for callin' you a liar, ma'am," Cash said, holding the ancient pistol steady, "but that old Mex didn't even have a gun."

"He keeps one in the barn," she said, and tore her eyes away from the barrel of that gun, from Cash entirely, and picked up her coffeepot again, righting it. "Besides," she added, "that old Colt you're brandishing isn't even loaded."

"Is, too!" he exclaimed. "I heard you tell Sheriff Granger!"

"Excuse me," she said, moving toward him. "I need to get the coffee."

He backed up a step, and she bent to the lower cupboard. He frowned at her. "Ma'am, I'm real sorry, but you're tryin' my patience. That old man hasn't got any gun, and this one's loaded for sure. Now, what I want you should do, is . . . Ma'am, would you kindly stand up while I'm talkin' to you?"

She stood, the coffee in one hand and her old butcher knife, the dull one, the one she'd been meaning to have Enrique or Julio sharpen, secreted along the other.

"That's better," Cash said. "What I want you to do is walk out the door, real ordinary-like, and the two of us are goin' to take us a stroll down to the barn."

"Horsefeathers," she said, her chin raised. "I just told you, that pistol isn't loaded."

"Cut it out!" Cash said, and desperation crept into his voice. "Is everybody in this town crazy? Look, lady, I don't want to hurt you. I just want to get out of here as fast as that horse can carry me."

With a shake of her head, she slid the bag of coffee beans onto the counter, next to the grinder, and looked him square in the eye. "Such a big lad to be such a wee coward," she said softly.

Cash's mouth set into a hard line. "I'll let that pass, but only 'cause you're a female."

"Go ahead," she said, undaunted. "Shoot me, if you truly believe I'd be stupid enough to put bullets in that gun with a houseful of children. Test it for yourself! Aim it at the ceiling or the floor if you're so set on chivalry that you wouldn't kill a woman yourself, but leave your dirty work to the Apaches!"

Cash was red in the face by this time, and she thought for a moment that he really would shoot her. But angrily, he swung the pistol to the side and fired. It went off, all right, just like she'd known that it would, and in the fraction of a second it took for surprise to flicker across Cash's countenance, she stepped behind him and brought the knife up hard against his throat.

"Oh, God, lady," he whispered.

"I imagine that will bring someone soon enough," she said, pressing blade to flesh. "Pistol on the table, please."

When he hesitated, she added, "I should do it if I were you. I may be a woman, but I'm a good bit older and a great deal meaner than you are. And trust me—I have much less to lose."

The gun fell from Cash's fingers. It clattered to the tabletop, dinging a pale chip into its shine.

"Do be careful!" she said.

"Nancy?" James and Melody were standing in the doorway, staring, holding the basket of eggs between them.

Her knees threatened to give way at any moment, but Nancy held the knife steady and said, "There you are, children. James, would you please set the eggs on the table, then remove that pistol? There's a good lad, point it down at the floor."

● ● ●

Dix and Enrique were just climbing through the patchwork of boards and into the mine when they heard the shot. Abandoning the lanterns in their haste, they sprinted toward the line of buildings, and with each step, Dix heard Enrique chant, "Soledad, no! Soledad!"

Enrique, who was hard and tough from laboring in the fields, ran faster than Dix, who was winded by the time they reached the barn. He glanced up to see old Julio, perched on the roof and frantically pointing down the street toward Nancy MacGregor's house. Dix put on a burst of extra speed, but Enrique still beat him there by three strides.

He skidded through the doorway to find Nancy calmly cracking eggs into a bowl while Cash and the children sat quietly at the table. Soledad was nowhere in sight, but Enrique was sputtering something in Spanish.

"Slow down," said Nancy. *Splat* went another egg into the bowl. "You know I can't understand when you go so fast, Enrique."

"What the hell's going on here?" Dix blurted. "Where's Soledad? Did she shoot somebody else?" He didn't see her anywhere.

"Hardly," Nancy said, and wiped her hands on her apron. "Cash put a new hole in my wall, but everything's fine now."

"What?" Dix roared, and Cash ducked his head.

"Calm down, for heaven's sake!" she said. "It's over! And it was my fault for—"

"Excuse please, *señor*," came a female voice from behind him. Quickly, he turned to discover Soledad, standing in the doorway. She wasn't armed—that was the first thing he looked for—but she was holding something wrapped in a cloth, and both the bundle and her arms were patched with pale streaks of blood.

"—leaving the pistol out," Nancy finished.

"Soledad!" cried Enrique, and went to her immediately. "Are you hurt, my dove, my angel?"

He tried to fold her into his arms, but she shrugged him off, saying, "What is wrong with you, Enrique? Are you crazy? You will make me drop the meat!"

"What meat?" asked a puzzled Enrique.

"The pronghorn you shoot!" Soledad said, rolling her eyes.

"Everybody shut up!" Dix hollered.

And blessed silence fell over the little adobe. A silence through which they all heard the dog barking and Julio shouting, his voice and the thuds of his sandaled feet upon the pale ground growing swiftly nearer. "They come!" he cried as he barreled in the door. "They are coming!"

7

Cash looked up and eyed the panting Julio. "Aw, he ain't got no gun at all, Miz MacGregor!" he said in disgust.

Dix ignored him. It was either that or shoot him. "Apache?" he asked quickly.

"Apache," whispered Soledad. "The Apache come."

"*Sí, patrón,*" said Julio. He was leaning against the wall, hands on his thighs. He held up two fingers. "*Dos,*" he said. "Leading an extra pony. They come from the north."

It was the same direction from which he and Yancy had come, the same direction in which he'd sent Yancy this morning. He hoped to God that they'd missed each other. He didn't dwell on it, though. There were more immediate things that needed tending.

"Nancy," he said, "get to the back of the house. Take Soledad. Barricade the windows as best you can, and get the kids under their beds. And be quiet."

The children scuffed from the room immediately, and the boy's eyes held something odd, something Dix couldn't identify. Soledad, however, didn't move so easily. She dropped her bundle of meat and backed toward a wall, muttering, "Burn, burn, burn . . ." Her hands, stained with pronghorn blood, were pressed to her cheeks.

"Come, Soledad," urged Nancy. "Now!"

Dix tossed his handgun to Julio. "Can you use that?"

The old man nodded and quickly checked the chambers.

"You got a firearm, Enrique?"

"At my house," he replied sorrowfully.

Dix went to the cupboards. "Where'd she put that old Navy?" he muttered.

"Top shelf," called Nancy. She was still trying to drag Soledad from the room.

"What about me?"

Nancy's gun in his hand, Dix turned to find Cash, holding out his arms. "You can't leave me cuffed, Sheriff!" he wailed beseechingly. "Not now! Gimme a gun!"

"Quiet!" Dix barked. He handed the pistol to Enrique just in time to see Soledad suddenly sprint from the room and disappear through the door in the rear. Nancy threw up her hands and followed.

"But I gotta have a chance!" cried Cash.

"You're going to get this rifle butt alongside your skull if you don't shut the hell up," Dix snarled, and brought up the rifle for emphasis. Cash pounded his fists on the table once, but he said no more.

"*Señor?*" Julio hissed. "What about Papagayo?"

Dix could hear him, still angrily barking in the distance. "Will he stay with those goats or come back here?"

"Stay with the goats, I think," Julio said, frowning. "But then, this is only what I think. For him, it is a hard thing to decide."

"You'd best pray he doesn't come in, then," Dix said. He'd seen Apaches spear a dog just for the sport of it. "Both you men, take a window."

Dix went to the door and closed it all but a hair. He peered though the opening while, in silence, they waited.

After a few minutes had passed, with Dix getting jumpier by the second and no sound except those distant barks, Enrique said softly, "You must forgive my Soledad, *Señor* Sheriff."

Dix didn't say anything. He'd been thinking about Yancy, out there, all alone.

"She . . . she has had a bad time. The Apaches, they killed her mother and her brother. She watched them burn alive, *señor.*"

Dix closed his eyes, pressed the lids together.

"She was eight when it happened," Enrique said softly, "and I do not know why they spared her. Who can say with these fiends?"

Dix opened his eyes again. There was still nothing outside, nothing. Quietly, he said, "Was that how she got scarred?"

"Sí," Enrique said, so sadly that it made Dix's heart hurt just to hear him. "They did not tie her to the wheels of the wagon with her mama and brother. They only held her down and put a burning branch to her little face, and they . . . they did something else, too. Something horrible, with a knife. I cannot talk about it. And they laughed while she screamed."

"I'm sorry," Dix said. That didn't half begin to cover it.

"She has always been a little crazy," Enrique said quietly. "But she was kind and good when we were married. I did not mind the scars. I did not mind that because of what those animals did, she could not bear my children. I loved her, *señor.* When we found Nancy, it was as if my Soledad had found a new purpose, you know?"

There was still nothing outside but the soft wind kicking up a haze of dust along the street. Even the dog had quieted to an occasional bark. He wondered if they were still far away, sitting their ponies and deciding what to do, or if they were already on the roof.

"You found Nancy?" he said, glancing at the ceiling. "What do you mean, you found her?" He'd broken out in a sweat, and quickly ran the back of his sleeve across his forehead. Why didn't the bastards do something?

"She has not told you?"

"Hasn't been much time for life stories."

"By the barn," hissed Julio, interrupting them.

The door opened the wrong way to allow Dix to see without sticking his head out, and he moved quickly to nudge Julio aside. He peered through the gun port in the shutter. Thank God these adobes had been built by men who expected the worst.

There were two Apaches, all right, and they had just emerged from the far side of the barn. One rode a strawberry roan and led a riderless gray. The second one sat a slab-sided pinto. They seemed engaged in conversation, unaware that they were a scant thirty feet from the grave of the companion they sought.

"Can you see any weapons?" Dix whispered to Enrique. His eyes were no good for details at this distance.

Enrique squinted. "The one on the roan has a rifle. The other has a spear. Maybe more. I cannot tell."

"If that's all they got and there's only two of 'em," piped up Cash, "why don't you just plug 'em from here?"

"I'm not going to tell you again," Dix said through clenched teeth.

"I was just sayin'," Cash muttered.

The one on the pinto was pointing to the roofs of the adobes, and his finger settled on their shelter. It was the smoke, of course. Nancy had been going to fix them breakfast. She'd lit a fire. He kicked himself for not thinking to warn her, and for not remembering to douse it first thing.

It was too late now.

The brave on the pinto urged his mount forward at a walk while the second brave pulled back, behind the shelter of the barn. While the men inside held their breaths, he rode quietly up the street, his pony's plodding hooves scuffing soft puffs of dust into the light breeze. About ten yards out, he came to a halt.

He called something in Spanish.

"What'd he say?" Dix asked. This was no time for guessing.

"He wishes to know if there is anyone here," came the reply.

"That's choice," Dix muttered beneath his breath. He went back to his original spot at the door. He had a good view of the brave. Lean and dressed in pale breeches, a tan shirt, and an orange headband, he was probably in his mid-twenties. He rode his pony with an Army bridle and somebody's good stock saddle, partially draped with a Mexican blanket.

"He's a real joker, this boy," Dix said. "Ask him what he wants."

Enrique jabbered in Spanish, and the Indian jabbered back.

"Well?"

"He says he is a friend of the white man. He says he and his companion would like some water."

"What a bunch'a horseshit!" exclaimed Cash.

This time, Dix didn't speak. He simply turned around, walked the three steps to Cash, and bashed him over the head with the butt of his rifle. The boy toppled forward, face first, onto the table.

"Tell them there's a well by the barn," Dix said. He hauled Cash's head up just long enough to make sure he was still alive. "Told you I wouldn't say it again," he muttered before he turned back to Enrique. "They can help themselves. Tell them we're friends of the Apache."

While Enrique translated, Dix hissed to Julio, "Can you see the near side of the barn from there?" When the old man nodded, he said, "Watch that his buddy doesn't try to sneak around it."

"I am already doing this, *señor,*" Julio said in disgust, as if he were annoyed Dix would think to ask him.

"Sorry," Dix said under his breath.

The brave had answered by this time, and Enrique said, "He wishes to know if there is any food in the house. He wants provisions."

"Provisions, my aunt Martha," Dix hissed. "He's tryin' to sweet-talk his way in here, or at least get us to open the door. If there were more of 'em, they wouldn't ask so nice." He paused for a moment. "Tell him we've got no food. Tell him we live off the land like he does. Tell him he can take a goat if he wants."

Julio exclaimed, "*¡Señor!*"

"Better a goat than you, my friend," Dix soothed.

Enrique had no more than started to translate when, from the back of the house, Dix heard Nancy cry, "Soledad! Dix! She's gone out the window!"

And before Dix could think what to do, the brave by the barn had reappeared again. He held something high, something that glinted brightly in the morning sun. He called to his friend.

Suddenly, Enrique shoved him out of the way with a cry of "Soledad, no!"

Dix fell back hard against the table's edge. Enrique threw the door wide and raced outside before Dix could regain his feet. "Idiot!" he bellowed, and raced toward the doorway, his rifle at the ready.

He got to it just in time to see Enrique swat the pistol from Soledad's hand and throw himself crossways in front of her, just in time to see the spear leave the Apache's hand and pierce Enrique's chest. And just in time to hear a gun discharge and see the young Apache tumble from his horse.

All this, before the pistol Enrique had knocked from Soledad's hand thudded into the dust.

The Indian pony wheeled and ran, dragging the dead Apache with him down across the old riverbed and out past the cornfield. To the accompaniment of Papagayo's distant but furious barks, the horse rocketed out onto the plain at a hard gallop, raising a trail of dust behind him.

The other brave fired from the sheltered edge of the barn. The slug tore a hole in the adobe not two feet from Dix. He felt the chips sting his face even as he dived back into the house, head first.

He felt Julio rip the Winchester from his fingers, heard two more shots boom out in rapid succession, and then heard Julio curse. He climbed to his feet, intending to get the damned rifle back, but Julio was shaking his head. Shrugging, he handed over the Winchester. "He is too far for this gun, *señor.*"

Dix stuck his head back outside to see the puff of dust, already headed for the southwest at a gallop. It veered to the east well beyond rifle range and met with the second dust trail, then stopped. The second brave was picking up his fallen companion. A few moments later, the horses were off again, their dust trail disappearing into the distance.

"Is Soledad all right?" Nancy breathed at his shoulder. He hadn't heard her come into the room. Then she said, "Oh, dear God. What happened to Cash? And where's Enrique?"

He was dead. She could scarcely believe this could happen to Enrique, but he was as dead as Ewan and Sarah and John, murdered by the same enemy. His eyes were empty and vacant, past saving by any human power.

The spear had passed through Enrique's heart, passed through his body and stabbed Soledad. In her case, it was only a slight wound, but she had lost consciousness nonetheless. It was a blessing, as far as Nancy was concerned. Had Soledad started to babble that nonsense again, Nancy would have been hard-pressed not to slap her across the mouth, and that would have been a heartless thing. Soledad couldn't help it.

Poor, sweet Enrique, she thought as Dix and Julio slowly carried him off toward the cemetery. He had become family, and he had saved her twice. The first time, he had saved her life. The second time, he had saved her soul.

She pulled a handkerchief from her skirt pocket. She blew her nose, then wiped away the tears. There would be time for grieving later. At the moment, there was Soledad to get into the house and see to, and then there was breakfast to cook.

Sometimes she heartily wished somebody else would be the woman for a little while. Let someone else do all the washing and cleaning, the sewing and cooking and canning. Let someone else do the worrying about these poor children and the garden and whether she'd get enough peppers or peas or tomatoes jarred up for the winter. Let someone else worry about the Apache.

No, that was wrong. Everybody was worried about the Apache. Everyone was scared. Everyone except Melody and James. Melody was barely aware of her surroundings, and James had seemed almost eager, although it was difficult to gauge emotions with that child.

"Please, dear God," she said in muttered prayer, "watch over that deputy who rode out this morning. Take him safely to find help. Take him swiftly."

And then, with a sigh, she bent and slid an arm beneath Soledad's shoulders. Nancy was strong, and she got Soledad to her feet with little trouble. By that time,

Soledad had come around just enough that she could move her legs a little, if by nothing more than instinct, and support part of her own weight. Slowly, Nancy moved her over the threshold of the little adobe.

Dix had dragged Cash over to the fireplace and cuffed him to a U-shaped bolt sticking from it, and Cash had regained consciousness in her absence. He was sitting up, his handcuffed arm stretched overhead, and rubbing his temple while the children silently watched. But then, the children were almost always silent, weren't they?

"Where'd the Apaches go?" he asked groggily. "How'd I get over here?" And then he pointed to the blood smear on Soledad's bodice. "What happened to her? What'd I miss?"

"More than you can know," she said, and helped Soledad past him, to her bedroom.

At Dix's request, Julio had taken the lead, and the two men had carried Enrique's body to the town's little graveyard. Now they were coming back from a short walk to the barn, where they had found two shovels and a pick, which they carried over their shoulders. The pale earth from last night's burial still clung to the edges of the shovels in powdery veils.

The cemetery wasn't much. Several tilting wooden crosses stood there, as well as a handful of small stone markers, their limestone melting and their crudely engraved words blurry. There were few weeds, though. Someone had been tending it. Probably Nancy or Soledad.

"Where?" asked Dix.

"Here, I think. Beside Juan Mondragon. I have heard Enrique speak of him often. They were *amigos*."

Dix drove the pick into the ground. The soil was harder than it was behind the barn, if that were possible, and he realized bleakly that this was going to take a while. He was glad Julio had talked him into bringing the pick.

"I am sorry, *Señor* Sheriff," Julio said as he shoveled away the dirt and rocks that Dix had loosened.

"What about?" Dix asked, and swung the pick again. There seemed to be so many things to be sorry for. He wished he'd had a chance to get to know Enrique better. He'd seemed like a good man.

"I am sorry I missed that Apache, the one by the barn," Julio replied thoughtfully. His stomach growled loudly. Dix's had been rumbling for the last hour or so.

"I think your gun, she shoots a little to the left," Julio went on. "I could file the sights, if you wish. I am not sorry I shoot the one by the house, though. I only wish that I had shot him a little sooner. But if I had got the one by the barn, then maybe they would have left us alone. What I mean, *señor,* is that they would not be coming back."

Obviously, everybody here knew how Apache justice operated. An eye for an eye and a tooth for a tooth. Preferably a lot of eyes for an eye.

Although, all in all, he couldn't say that the whites were much better. They just pretended to be.

He kept the pick swinging rhythmically. Sweat glued his shirt to his back like a second skin, rolled into his eyes. He blinked it away, ignored it. "You've got nothing to be sorry for. I should have locked Soledad up. Don't know where she got that damned gun."

Julio shoveled dirt from the grave. "Nancy, she keeps a spare pistol in her bedroom cupboard. Enrique gave it to her a long time ago. Soledad must have known. She must have taken it down and climbed from the back window, and . . ." He shrugged. "I am sorry that Soledad is crazy, too. I am sorry for Enrique. But I am not sorry for his bravery."

It had been a foolish stunt that got Enrique killed, but

Dix didn't say that. Most acts of sudden bravery, in his experience, were gallant but stupid gestures, and nine times out of ten, their perpetrators ended up dead. Enrique had sacrificed himself to keep the breath in a madwoman, and in doing so, he had reduced their fighting numbers by a third. It was just him and Julio, now. The way he saw it, Cash didn't count.

So he didn't answer. He simply grunted and carried on with his attack upon the earth.

"I wonder what it was," Julio said. "The shiny thing he held up. Did you see?"

Dix stopped working. He stood up and pressed a hand into the small of his back. "Yes, I saw," he said. He knew exactly what it had been: a disk of silver, hammered thin and about three inches across, with a hole in the middle for a leather thong.

"The Apache we buried last night was wearing it," he said flatly. We must have lost it when we were draggin' him out back of the barn. He paused. "Like I said, Julio, there's nothing for you to be sorry about. They'd be coming back to get us, one way or the other."

They worked in silence until they were about two feet down. Julio brought water, and the two men crouched beside the grave, sweating and panting, gulping comparatively cool water and splashing it over their faces.

Julio rose first and took the pick from Dix. "My turn," he said. He stepped down into the grave.

Dix stood up and pulled out his pocket watch. Only ten-fifteen. It didn't seem possible. He glanced up at the sky, just to make sure his watch hadn't stopped. It hadn't. The sun was still in the east.

He looked out across the riverbed and saw the goats foraging in the distance and the little blurry speck of red that was Papagayo. He saw the cornfield and, behind it a patch of tall, thick grass he hadn't noticed before. Hay, he supposed. Enrique must have hauled a lot of water, hauled it day and night.

What were these people going to do without him?

But he saw no sign of returning Apache. He didn't know how far away the main band was camped, but he hoped it was distant enough to delay their attack until tomorrow. He thought again about Yancy, out there on Dasher. He thought about the old mine shaft.

There came a soft crunching of gravel between the impacts of Julio's pick, and Dix turned to find Nancy walking toward him. A folded blanket was in her arms.

"Come and eat," she said when she reached them. She shook out the blanket, shooed the flies away from the corpse, then shrouded Enrique's body. Dix helped her place stones around the edges to hold it down. The wind was beginning to kick up again.

"Vaya con Dios, mi amigo," he heard her whisper before she rose.

8

Dix and Julio ate like wolves, then went back to the grim business of grave digging. They were finished by noon, and Nancy and the children knelt by the grave. Nancy brought a few pale and wilting wildflowers. Soledad didn't come, and Nancy said she was sleeping.

"She doesn't know he's dead," she confided to Dix after Julio, his hat held over his heart, had said a few emotional words in Spanish. "These spells she has leave her exhausted and confused. She may not even remember where she is until tonight."

His sombrero in place once more, Julio picked up the shovels. "This is true, *señor,*" he said ruefully. Sweat made tracks down his face, following the paths of deep wrinkles. "My *dinero* would be on tomorrow morning. It is sad."

Nancy reached over and took the old man's arm, squeezing it briefly. The children waited silently for her, holding hands. The gathering breeze whipped at the little girl's homespun dress and snapped the boy's britches.

Dix felt that he should say something to them, something comforting, but he had no idea what those words might be. Nobody else seemed to have talked to them about Enrique. But he wasn't good with children, at least, he hadn't been since Clara died. He hadn't tried much afterward, because the pain was too great. It had been a very long time.

He'd likely make a fool of himself no matter what he said, but he resigned himself to that fact and knelt down. He tried the little girl first. "I'm real sorry about Enrique, honey. I know he was a good friend to you."

"Melody doesn't speak," Nancy said from above him. He didn't look at her, though. He was studying Melody.

The girl, who he figured to be about nine years old, didn't look stupid or mulish, merely distracted. He raised his hand and snapped his fingers beside her ear. Her eyes flicked toward it almost imperceptibly, but he saw.

"She's not deaf," he said, still studying her. Her big blue eyes stared not at him, but just past his shoulder. "Does she make any sounds?"

The boy turned his head toward Dix. His eyes were as big and blue as his sister's, his hair as fair. "She will," he said quietly and steadily but with a fierce determination. "She'll talk again once we're home. They're going to come back and get us. You'll see."

And with that, the two turned and began to scuff back down the street toward Nancy's house.

Dix stood up. "What's he mean, when they're home again? Does he figure their folks are still alive?"

Nancy shook her head. "No," she whispered sadly. "I think he means the Apaches."

Before Dix could ask her anything else, she was gone, scurrying after the children.

"Early last spring, the Indian came. It was after we had planted the corn," Julio was saying. He and Dix had returned to the mine, and had just crawled through the gap in the boarded entrance.

Dix grabbed a lantern and turned up the wick. He scowled. "An Apache? Soledad must have been tied up someplace."

Julio shrugged. "I don't remember where she was. Sleeping, maybe. Or in the garden."

"And you say he just dropped the kids and rode off?"

"*Sí*. It was very strange, *señor*. He was alone, with no other riders. An old Apache, very old." Julio leaned against the mine's wall wearily, a lantern suspended from his hand. "He came in the early morning, when Papagayo had just taken the goats out. He dropped the children from his horse like . . . like they were a buck he had shot. And then he just rode away. The boy, James, he ran after him for a while. But he was weak and soon gave up. Enrique chased him down and brought him back."

Sighing, Dix shook his head. He would never understand why the Apache did a damned thing. They'd probably murdered the children's folks. Probably lopped off that boy's fingers, too. They had likely kept the kids for a year or two or three, found out they ate too much to keep during hard times, and then turned around and dropped them off like dirty laundry at the nearest civilized settlement.

But if the children were too great a drain on the Apaches, why take them in the first place? Why leave them at Regret instead of trading them to another band? Why not just slit their throats?

"The kids tell you their names?"

"James did, after a while," Julio said. "He said that Melody was his sister, but he could not remember the last name. I think they were with the Apache a long time. Nancy was made much better when they came, but Soledad? Soledad was much worse. You see how Nancy watches the children so close when Soledad is around?"

Dix nodded. Come to think of it, every time Soledad was in the room—when she was having a bad spell, anyway—Nancy always had those kids right next to her. Or tucked behind her skirts.

"Soledad tried to kill them only a week after they came to us."

Something gripped Dix deep in his belly, a familiar mixture of loathing and lost hope and helplessness, and he said, "Kill them?"

"Enrique found her lifting Melody into the well. It is a long drop to the water. Soledad, she was laughing. She said, 'Enrique, water puts out fire. I will drown these little heathens before they burn us. Tell Nancy she can sleep safely.' Enrique, he was blessed with the patience of a saint, but he had to strike Soledad. It made him very sad."

Dix turned away, the ancient pain flooding back on him once more. Madwomen murdering children. Poor mad Ramona. Poor little Clara. She would have been twenty-five if she had lived. No, twenty-six. How could he have forgotten a thing like that?

He started down the tunnel, checking supports and knocking down cobwebs as he went, and trying to pull his mind away from the past, from that little white-shuttered house engulfed in flames. He'd built it for Ramona with his own two hands, built it with lumber and adobe bricks and paint and nails and dreams. He'd carried her across its threshold, the both of them laughing.

Now he only remembered it aflame, with his wife and daughter inside, and two men holding him back, saying, "It's too late, Dix, it's too late."

"The little girl," he said, forcing himself to the present. "Melody. Has she ever spoken?"

"No," said Julio. "The *muchacha* was silent from the first. It was a month at least before we found out she could hear, but she still does not speak. I had thought that maybe they had taken her tongue, but I looked. It is still there. *Señor,* I have never heard James make so great a speech as he did today. It worries me."

"I wish you'd just call me Dix."

The wind suddenly pushed at the mine's entrance with a high-pitched howl, and both men turned back toward it, startled.

"Great," muttered Dix, grounded firmly in the here and now once more. "Looks like we're in for another bitch of a storm tonight."

Julio nodded slowly. "Maybe sooner."

Dix looked about him. They'd only walked about thirty feet back into the shaft, but what he'd seen of it seemed to be in fairly decent condition. He walked about four yards deeper and found that the shaft, which was gradually going downhill, bent to the left. The woman and children—and Cash—would be safe here. The safest he could make them, anyway.

He looked no further. He walked back up to Julio and said, "We'd best start gettin' ready. Guns, ammunition. Blankets, extra lanterns. Fill everything with water that'll hold it."

Julio nodded and started toward the dusty light at the tunnel's mouth, stopping to crush something underfoot on the way.

"A spider," he said in disgust. "Black widow."

"Your eyes are a lot better than mine, *amigo.*"

"They are thick in here. I think maybe the water is still in the shaft."

Dix, who had been squinting to see if there were more spiders, looked up. "What water?"

"It is why they closed the mine," said Julio. "It flooded, and they could not pump it fast enough. The river runs underground here, and they dug down past its level. I thought everyone knew that. But then," he added with a shrug, "it has been a long time. The moisture brings the bugs, and the bugs bring the spiders."

"Perfect," muttered Dix. Somehow, though, the prospect of a legion of black widows seemed far less horrendous than the prospect of Apaches getting hold of Nancy MacGregor.

When they reached the opening and once more climbed out into the brash light of day, Dix paused.

"I'd best get the rest of these boards pried off," he said, studying them. The wind, which had risen a good bit just since they went into the mine, pushed at his back and snapped his shirt and trouser legs. "Don't want those Apaches gettin' any ideas about settin' them on fire and smoking us out."

"Bueno," said Julio and started toward the town, but he stopped after only a few steps. *"Señor* Sheriff?" he called. "What about my goats?"

"Best leave them outside tonight, Julio," Dix said. "Let 'em wander and spread out. And call me Dix."

"But—"

"Better you have to spend a day lookin' for them than they end up over an Apache cook fire."

Julio heaved a sigh. "Papagayo? And the horse?"

"Reckon I'll leave Chunk in the barn. They might swipe him—and if they do, I'm gonna have me one cranky deputy—but I don't think they'll kill him. I want the dog in here, with us, and I want him on a rope. If this morning was any indication, he'll give the first alert, but I don't want him chargin' out."

"Sí, patrón."

Dix sighed. Julio was never going to call him by his given name.

He watched as Julio shuffled off into the wind, and then he got busy with the boards. As he ripped them down and tossed them inside, intending to carry them deeper into the mine and away from keen eyes and clever minds, he was thinking about Yancy and wondering if he was still loping back to Gushing Rain, or if he'd been cut down by one of those braves that had come this morning.

By two-thirty that afternoon, Yancy had covered a good twenty miles of rough terrain by alternately loping and jogging Dasher. Over the flat parts, at least. He was making excellent time, and he was doing it without breaking the horse's wind.

He was glad Dix had insisted he take Dasher. His Chunk was a damn fine mount, all right, but he was a sprinter. You couldn't beat him over a quarter mile. At least, nobody'd been able to since Yancy won him in a card game, back when he first came to deputy for Dix.

But Chunk had less stamina over the long haul. Yancy figured he and Dasher could make it to town by nightfall or a little after, barring catastrophe, and once he got there, he was going to see that ol' Dasher had the best rubdown in the history of the Gushing Rain livery.

He patted the horse on the neck. Sweating, but not lathered. Good.

He reined in Dasher and stepped down from the saddle, gave him a rub on the forehead, pulled out the nosebag, and pulled down the water. Nickering softly, the horse pushed at him with his nose.

"I'm pourin' as fast as I can, you big galoot," Yancy said good-naturedly. "Not too much, now."

Once again, he went over his plans to collect a posse. He'd go to Old Man Peterson first. He might be a banker, but he also owned a cattle spread north of town. He could send men even if he was too old and too rich to come himself. Dick Johnson would come, he was pretty sure. Pete Halstead and Ronnie White would be itching to get after some Apache.

He had come up with a list of twenty-four men, altogether, that he thought might be convinced, one way or the other, to ride out with him. Five or six of them would come right off. The rest he'd have to shame or blackmail into it, but he thought he could do that. He knew which strings to pull and what to whisper into each man's ear. Being the town deputy made a man privy to all sorts of things he'd never speak about. Except when there were lives involved, and especially when one of those lives was Dix's. That changed everything.

Still, he worried. Twenty-four men was quite a few, but they'd be reluctant for the most part, and he had no way of knowing what they'd be going up against. He was no Indian fighter.

Personally, he could sit around all day and trade tall tales with the Papago Indians. They were semi-nomadic farmers, and good people. Once a year they came to a place not far from Gushing Rain, a place where there was seepage water part of the year, to grow squash and corn and such. He'd gotten to be good friends with a few of them. It was out of his and Dix's jurisdiction, but the Papago knew they could come to Dix or him if they had trouble with anybody, white or otherwise.

Apache, on the other hand, scared the holy bejesus out of him. He wasn't ashamed of it any more than he was ashamed of having a sound mind. He figured they'd scare the bejesus out of any sane man.

He'd seen no sign of either Indians or whites during his journey, and as he sparingly watered Dasher, he kept his eyes moving from hilltop to hilltop. You never could tell. A man alone out here was taking a big risk, no matter how good his reasons for traveling solo. Apaches, rattlesnakes, bandits—both white and Mexican—and the damn weather: They were all against a fellow on his own.

Well, he supposed they were always against you, even

if you traveled in numbers. But if you had company, you at least had somebody to commiserate with.

"That's enough, fella," he said to the bay, who was lipping at the now-empty nosebag.

The wind had been kicking up over the last two hours. He sure hoped he wouldn't have to fight it on the tail end of the journey. Maybe he could outride the dang storm, he mused as he put the nosebag away. The wind nearly took it, but he snatched it back in time and tucked it down in the saddlebag.

"Maybe we're just on the edge of this she cat, Dasher," he said. "Mayhap we'll just ride out the other side."

Of course, the sky had already begun to change. Dirty-nickel clouds were beginning to lower. That sickly yellow light hadn't moved in yet, but he could see the first tinges of it in the clouds. And all around him, the brush was beginning to dance.

But maybe he could make it. Maybe he'd even get to town and get the posse ready before dark. He'd wait until he was about two miles from town, he decided, then open up Dasher all the way.

"Mama always said you were a born optimist, Yancy Wade," he muttered, and put his hand on the saddle horn.

He stepped back up on Dasher and urged him into a soft jog once again. That was the pattern he'd established. Water, jog, lope, then an extended lope, but not a gallop. Then back down to a jog for a while, then stop and water again. It seemed to be doing the trick.

Two miles later, just after he'd sighted Spider Rock and had congratulated himself on finally seeing something familiar, Dasher stumbled at the lope. Before Yancy could pull him up—or even think to, what with his mind full of Dix, and the Apaches pouring in—the horse went all the way down.

Yancy went sailing before Dasher hit his knees, then his

side, and skidded over the rocky ground. They both came to a stop in roughly the same place, and Yancy ducked fast and rolled to the side to avoid a pistoning hoof.

He checked himself quickly to make certain he hadn't busted his dang-fool neck or maybe a leg, but outside of his bandaged forearm and side, he guessed he was all right. He suspected he was going to have one helluva bruise on his right hip, though.

Dasher, on the other hand, wasn't doing so well. Alternately swearing and soothing, and all the time ducking hooves, Yancy finally got the horse untangled from his own reins and to his feet.

"Easy, easy," he murmured, then clucked and led Dasher forward a few steps.

"Aw, crud!" he wailed when the horse favored his right foreleg. Quickly, he stooped and checked it, running practiced hands from hoof to knee and back again, and then up, toward the shoulder. He breathed a sigh of relief when he determined the leg wasn't broken, just badly wrenched. The horse's knees were pretty skinned up, though, and the skid had taken some of the hide off his right hip.

"What'd you have to go and do that for, Dasher?" he complained bitterly as he began to strip off the bay's tack. "Jeez Louise, you're usually such a surefooted son of a bitch! What'd you step in, anyway? Don't you know we gotta help Dix? Don't you know there's probably about a thousand Apache ready to thunder down on him and those poor folks right now?"

The horse couldn't carry him, and Yancy had no time to baby him along and lead him back to town. He brushed grit away from the horse's injuries as best he could. And then, his own bruised hip hurting more with each passing second, he piled Dasher's saddle, bedroll, and saddlebags next to a rock. He pulled some jerky from the bags and stuck it in his pocket, clipped the canteen to his belt, shook out his bedroll, and stuck one blanket under his arm. He'd need it if this wind kept on coming.

He was pretty sure it would.

He emptied the last of his canvas water bag into a nose-bag and held it while the horse drank. Dasher would do better turned loose than he would tied or hobbled, where he'd be easy prey for coyotes or cougars.

"You'd best not wander too far," he said as the horse lipped up the last of the water. "Anything happens to you, and this time Dix won't stop at shootin' me in the ass. Anything happens to me," he added dismally, "and Dix and all those folks down there . . ."

He let the sentence trail off, unfinished. He didn't want to think about that.

With fresh purpose, he tucked the empty nosebag beneath the saddle and turned himself toward Spider Rock. Doing his best to ignore his throbbing hip, he gamely began to make his way north.

Dasher limped after him for almost a half a mile.

9

By five o'clock, the tunnel was stocked with water and food. Nancy had fed them all again at about four o'clock, and she had killed and fried up three hens to add to the baskets of biscuits and jars of honey and fruit preserves and jarred tomatoes and corn that she'd hauled down the shaft. Dried goat meat went, too, and the crisp fried corn tortillas that Julio loved so much, plus every vessel in town, filled with water. And two filled with limeade, which she'd made from the fruit of the one scraggly tree out back.

No one had laughed at her for making so many trips. No one knew how long it would be before help came.

If it came.

Besides, there was a good chance that her larder wouldn't survive the Apaches, even if they did.

She had packed and carried the food—or passed it off to Dix or Julio to carry—as well as trooped through the tunnel with a flaming torch, exterminating every black widow she could find with a whoosh and a pop. She had made certain that Soledad wasn't up to mischief and kept an eye on Cash and the children.

Cash, at least, seemed to have developed a healthy respect for her. He had almost cowered when she'd cleaned and cut up the hens for frying with her big butcher knife, and he had kept his usual chatter down to, "Yes ma'am," "No, ma'am," and "Thank you, ma'am."

And always, she kept glancing toward the southern horizon. Dix had told her that he didn't know how far away the main band of Apaches were camped, but that he believed they wouldn't attack until morning. She'd been nervous as a cat all day, but she was beginning to believe him.

It would be dark before sundown, at any rate. She had already lit a lantern and turned up the wick, for the sky was well on its way to a sooty black. It reminded her of the skies back in Pittsburgh, the days when there was no wind to carry away the smoke from the factories and mills. She'd thought she'd left that behind. And the land all around had a dim and sickly yellow look to her eyes, as if she were wearing amber-tinted glasses and couldn't take them off.

And then there was the wind. How she hated it! Over the last few years, she'd grown to think of it as an entity, an evil personality. It came in the night to flatten her garden, to rattle her door and shove dirt through the shutters, to blast at the walls of her house, and to keep her awake with its infernal howling. This time of year, it seemed she was always cleaning up after the last duststorm or preparing for the next one.

Right now it was storming. She could hear the booms of distant, dry thunder reverberating. It wasn't blowing as badly as it would be in an hour's time nor so furiously as it would rage two hours from now. She knew its habits. She knew its patterns. But the wind was such that her next trip to the mine shaft would be her last. On the previous trip, it had threatened to use her skirts for a sail and blow her to Sonora.

Julio had already taken Soledad to the mine. She was still nonsensical but thankfully nonviolent, and he had carried her tiny body out the door, her skirts wildly whipping about his white cotton trousers like a black pirate's flag.

Cash, too, was gone. Dix had come to retrieve him. He'd disengaged the handcuffs from the iron bolt in the fireplace, which he'd judged the only thing in the house that couldn't be worked or broken free, and set off into the wind with Cash complaining loudly.

She took off her apron and folded it neatly over the back of a chair.

"All right, children," she said. She kept her tone light and cheery, as if they were all about to have a great adventure. "Let's go while there's still some light to see by, shall we? James?"

His sister at his side, he sat at the table, hands quietly folded.

"Bring that book along. I'll read to you in the mine."

He didn't budge.

"James? Come along and bring your book. If you don't like that one, get another, but do hurry."

Still, he sat.

Nancy moved to his side and quietly slid the storybook into her skirt pocket. It was old and battered, and some of the pages were missing, but she'd thought the children liked it. Perhaps the strain of the day was working on James and Melody.

The Lord knew, it was working on her.

She almost put her hand on James's shoulder, then hesitated. He hated to be touched. At least, he always shrugged away. Well, this time, maybe he'd shrug right out of his chair. She brought her hand to rest lightly on the back of his neck.

He stood immediately and whirled to face her. "No," he

said in a quiet voice. His small hands, balled into fists, were the only things that belied his anger.

How could she get through to this child? Sometimes she thought a million years would not be enough.

"The Apaches are coming," he said. "Leave us here."

"I can't do that, James."

"Why?"

Nancy bit at the inside of her cheek. "Because," she said, doing her best to hold her voice to an even tone, "we're all going up to the old mine." Any other boy, any normal boy, would have tried everything under the sun to explore its secrets. James had barely looked toward it in all the months since he'd come to her.

"It'll be like a picnic," she urged. "I've made fried chicken and limeade and—"

"No," said James, cutting her off. His blue eyes betrayed no emotion. "You're going to hide from the Apaches. You think they're going to kill us."

She sat down and simply looked at him. After a moment, she quietly said, "And what do you think is going to happen if we don't go to the shaft, James?"

He studied her calmly, coldly, as if she were an insect pinned to a collector's board, and he started to open his mouth to answer.

He never did. Just at that moment, the door banged open with a huge rush of wind. Dix staggered in, shouting, "Come on, Nancy! She's blowin' up!"

The sky had gone nearly black in the few minutes she'd been inside, and her little front room was suddenly filled with flying grit and twigs and dust. She leapt to her feet immediately and wrapped Melody in one of the two blankets she'd kept back for just this purpose. She shook out the second one and draped it around James's shoulders.

Defiantly, he pushed it off. It blew across the room.

"No," he said. She could barely hear him over the howl

of the wind. The storm was rolling in too fast, too mean, and it frightened her.

Almost before she realized it, Dix had come around the table and snagged James's blanket from the floor. "Can you carry Melody?" he shouted over the wind, and in one quick motion, dropped the blanket back around James and scooped him up.

James struggled, lashing out with arms and legs, and Dix barked, "Hold still, boy," and gave him a little shake. James went limp.

By this time, Nancy had picked up Melody, who hung like a rag doll in her arms. Dix grabbed the lantern, and she followed him to the door.

"Hang onto the back'a my belt!" he shouted before he pulled his neckerchief up over his nose and mouth.

She readjusted Melody's weight, hurriedly pulled the blanket over the girl's face, then hooked two fingers through one of Dix's belt loops. "All right!" she called, "I'm ready!" and they marched out into the storm, forgetting entirely to close the door.

Without Dix, she soon realized, she would have been wandering for hours. She couldn't make out anything more than five feet from her nose through this blow. She ducked her head, shielding her face as best she could, and followed him blindly.

The wind eddied and gusted around the structures of the town, peppered and stung her head and neck with bits of detritus, sailed parts of old boards past her head, perilously close. Sometimes it threatened to topple her over on her side. Other times, it shoved at her back with the force of a charging bull, and she was thrown forward, into Dix. Her legs were continually tangled in her skirts, and twice she nearly went down. But Dix kept moving, slow but steady. He was a rock.

At last they reached the mine's mouth. Ten feet inside

it, Nancy let Melody slither to the ground. Her arm had gone numb from the weight of the child, and her skull was aching—as much from the pelting it had taken, as from the unrelenting noise of the wind.

Wordlessly, they crept around the long table that the men had carried from Enrique and Soledad's house and had set on its side, crossways in the tunnel. It would give them some shelter from bullets and arrows, Dix had said, and give them a better place to shoot from. Julio was already crouched on the other side of it, his arm around the dog.

Poor Papagayo looked a wee bit confused, she thought, and she smiled in spite of herself. He probably didn't understand why he couldn't bring his goats along.

Julio stood up and accompanied them down the tunnel, his lantern in one hand and the dog's rope leash in the other.

They rounded the turn in the shaft, and by then the wailing wind was distant enough so that Nancy could hear herself think. She stopped well away from the little group that had gathered there and shook out her skirts, then wiped her face and neck with her handkerchief. It felt like she was sandpapering them. She'd have given anything for a good, long bath.

But still, there were three lanterns lit in the little place she had made, and it glowed warmly. Soledad sat on a blanket against one wall, rocking herself slowly and staring dumbly into space. Cash, his handcuffs removed at last, was slouched against a support beam opposite her and a little farther down, but he came to attention when he saw Dix.

"I didn't run off, see?" he said defensively, and then held out his hands. "Julio said you said it was okay."

Dix nodded curtly and banged his hat against his leg. Dust billowed.

The children sat down between buckets of water and boxes of ammunition.

"Am I a free man?" Cash asked. There was a small note of hope in his voice.

But Dix replied, "Nope. You're on the honor system, that's all."

Nancy said, "The storm's different tonight." She was studying Soledad. It was too long for her to be like this, so vacant. Something was wrong. Well, more wrong than usual. Maybe it was just the wind. "It's strange," she added.

Dix said, "Sure came up all of a sudden, all right."

"It will rain," Julio announced with confidence.

"It's too early in the season to rain, Julio," Nancy said softly.

Julio turned and started back up the shaft. "It will rain," he said over his shoulder.

Twenty-three miles to the north, on a stretch of open and featureless desert, Yancy was huddled beneath a thin, brown blanket.

He had long ago lost his way in the dark, and finally sat where he stood. No sense moving when he didn't know what he was moving toward.

It had taken him a good ten minutes just to get the blanket fixed right. The wind kept taking it. It was nearly ripped from his hands several times, but he finally managed to rig it right and get the edges of it tucked under him all the way around. His legs crossed Indian style, his torso bent forward over his legs, the blanket wrapped him like a cocoon.

He figured that he must look pretty goddamn strange, like a big brown boulder. If there had been anyone to see him through this bitch of a blow, anyway. Which there wasn't.

His arm was pounding beneath the bandage, and his side didn't feel too good, either. Damn that Soledad, anyway! She had no business running around with a rifle. And his hip hurt like a bastard. He'd been limping more with every step. Sitting was almost worse.

Still, he reckoned it couldn't be as bad as what Dix and the others were going through. He wondered if the Apache had come down on them yet, or if they'd wait till morning. That would be a hell of a thing to live with, the waiting, the thinking about it. He worried about them, and he worried about old Dasher, all alone in this gale.

Dasher'd be all right, he told himself. Horses knew how to get through weather. He hoped.

"If ol' Dix makes it through this," he muttered into the screech of wind, "I'm gonna give him all my pies and cookies for a week. Maybe two. Even if Miss Annie brings another one'a those good marble cakes'a hers, he can have it."

Despite his lowered profile, the wind still pushed at him, shoved at him, stabbed and battered him through the thin blanket with sailing tumbleweeds and little bits of cactus, pelted him with tiny pebbles and sticks. It was a constant struggle to stay upright. If he let the wind tilt him enough, it would steal his blanket, and then where would he be?

He had been huddled in this manner for roughly an hour. He wished he had thought to bring more blankets. Hell, he wished he'd thought to bring a hole to crawl into.

Lightning flashed so close that it lit his clenched fists right through the blanket and shocked his stinging eyes. Directly on its heels boomed thunder so loud that the sound stabbed his ears.

Without thinking, he brought his hands up to cover them, shouting, "Stop it, just stop it!"

And the wind stopped, just like that.

Having no wind to lean against, Yancy fell over on his side. Beneath the blanket, he cocked his head. Slowly, his hands slid from his ears.

"I didn't mean stop the world, Lord," he whispered, thinking for a half second that the Almighty had actually listened to him at long last, and had just decided to call a halt to the whole planet.

But then he heard it: the patter of rain on dry ground, soft at first, then quickly escalating into a torrent.

"Aw, crud," he muttered.

Stiffly, he disengaged himself from the blanket, got to his feet, and tucked it under his arm. He still couldn't see anything, but he was soaked through almost immediately. The air, once full of flying things, was now a nearly solid sheet of water, cold water, that came straight down. The huge drops drummed at his hat and hurt like hell when they hit an exposed area of skin. They didn't feel too good on the covered parts, either.

He stood there in the pelt of rain, trying to ignore the pain in his hip while he waited for the next lightning flash. When it came, with the thunder nearly shaking him out of his boots, he glimpsed Spider Rock again. If he could just make it that far, he could find shelter in the boulders at its base.

If he didn't drown first.

If lightning didn't strike and sizzle him into a grease spot on the pooling ground.

With difficulty, he shook out the soaking blanket and draped it over his shoulders. It was a thin barrier against the hammering raindrops, but it was something, anyway.

Blindly, haltingly, he began to move in the direction of Spider Rock, correcting his path to the left or to the right each time the lightning flashed again. Water coursed from his hat brim, and his soaked britches made it feel like he was trudging through wet mortar.

When he stepped in a hole that buried his leg to the knee in cold, muddy sludge and toppled him, face first, into a dancing puddle of water, he swore mightily, then quickly stopped himself.

"Don't listen to me, God," he shouted into the storm, suddenly fearful that a swarm of locusts or a rain of frogs would be next on the agenda. The rain pelted down even harder than before, if that were possible, and it was cold, so cold.

"I was just talkin', all right?"

Lightning flashed again, illuminating the terrain around him in a harsh, unearthly light, and the thunder boomed mightily.

"The Lord spake," he muttered. His words rose up in a cloud of vapor, quickly tattered by gigantic raindrops. "And the Lord sayeth, get your sorry ass movin', Yancy Wade."

He pulled himself up out of the mire, wrapped the muddy blanket around him, and started limping toward Spider Rock once again.

10

"**I still don't** see why we had to come in here tonight," Cash said around a mouthful of fried chicken. It was his fourth piece. "Why couldn't we wait till morning?"

"You know why," Dix said. "Nancy, I believe this is about the best hen I've had in a coon's age." It was, too, no offense to the culinary skills of Yancy's crew of female admirers.

"And stop that!" he said to Cash. He reached over and thumped the kid's hand before he could snag another piece. He always went for the damned white meat! "That's got to last us."

Cash looked honestly chagrined. "Sorry, Sheriff," he said, then, "Sorry, ma'am. It was so toothsome, I guess I forgot myself." He wiped his hands on his britches while Soledad stared blankly.

"It's quite all right, Cash," Nancy said, and smiled at him.

Dix had noticed that Cash had been pussyfooting around Nancy ever since she'd got the upper hand with him this morning. She'd told Dix about it later, although she hadn't spent more than two or three sentences with the telling. He liked that about her. Right to the point, and not a whole lot of fuss in the getting there.

But Cash must have been good and scared, all right. A female, holding a knife to Cash Malone's throat! Some desperado. Dix wished he'd seen that.

But at the moment, he seemed to be relaxing a little. Maybe he'd figured out that Nancy MacGregor only bit when she was threatened. The rest of the time, she was as smooth and soft as kitten's fur.

He admired that, too.

Dix leaned forward and dropped the chicken leg, cleaned right down to the bone and gristle, into the little pail Nancy had provided for just that purpose. She thought of everything, that woman.

He said, "Cash, now that your belly's full, why don't you go up the shaft and relieve Julio. Tell him to come back and get some grub."

Cash looked shocked. "Me?"

"I'm trusting you," Dix said. He didn't add that the wind was still raging something godawful outside, and he doubted that Cash would be able to find his way ten feet from the tunnel—let alone to the barn—without getting himself hopelessly lost.

Cash asked, "I . . . I don't s'pose I can have my gun back."

Dix reached to the side and slid Cash's pistol from beneath a stack of blankets. Without a word, he handed it over, butt first.

Cash took it and stared at it, then at Dix. "I, uh, thanks," he said at last. He got to his feet, stepped over Soledad's outstretched legs, and started up the tunnel, back to where the wind was a screech rather than a low, moaning hum.

"Cash?" Dix called before the kid had gone three steps.

"You might want to load that first. You got plenty on your belt."

Cash grinned at him sheepishly. "Yessir."

"He's a good boy at heart," said Nancy softly. Melody was half asleep in the crook of her arm, her thumb in her mouth. James sat several feet away, staring at the cover of an unopened storybook.

"I suppose," Dix said. It pleased him that she could still talk kindly about Cash after he'd pulled a gun on her. Most women—most men, too—would have demanded Cash's blood. She knew how to read people, all right. At least, she'd read Cash the same way he had. And tomorrow they'd need all the help they could get. It wouldn't hurt to do a little confidence building—both his in Cash and Cash's in himself—tonight.

He said, "Just wish I knew why he did it."

"Which thing?"

He looked at her. "Robbed the bank, of course. Reckon he's pulled a few gimcrack stunts since then, too, hasn't he?"

She smiled. "I knew he wouldn't hurt me. He's all bluff and false bravado, but I'd wager there's a good boy underneath. It'd only take a little push to make him a good man."

She said it like she expected that push to come from Dix. But he had no intention of being Cash's—or anybody else's for that matter—mentor or soul savior. As sheriff, he was just supposed to bring in lawbreakers, that was all.

Instead, he said, "This morning, just before . . . just before Enrique ran out the door, he said something. He said they found you." Enrique had told him some, and so had Julio, but he wanted the whole story.

"Yes, they did, he and Julio," she replied matter-of-factly. "Would you care for more limeade? I'm sorry there isn't coffee."

He held out his mug. Strange woman, this Nancy Mac-

Gregor. Smart as a whip, but strange. Of course, there wasn't a regular person in the whole town.

"Where'd they find you? Were you lost on the desert?"

Carefully, she poured out more of the sweet, pulpy liquid. "In a manner of speaking. We were in a wagon train, headed for California. It wasn't big, just three wagons and our own. Mine and Ewan's. And the children's, of course."

She capped the jar and set it aside. "John was seven and Sarah was ten. Of course, that was three years ago. Sarah's thirteenth birthday would have been last week."

Would have been. The words cut him like a blade.

Someone else kept track of lost birthdays, of lost children, of what might have been. Suddenly, he didn't want her to go on.

But she did. "We were a bit south of here. We'd been traveling the old Mormon Battalion Trail." She smiled. "Ewan said he'd be able to tell just where that trail was from miles and miles away. It was all the broken glass shining along both its sides, of course. Decades of discarded bottles. We'd just left it the week before and cut to the west. Clarence Webster—he was our unofficial leader—had it on good authority that there was a more expedient passage in that direction."

"Stop," whispered Dix. He didn't want her to tell it.

But his murmur was lost in the sound of the wind, and she didn't hear him. "It was in the afternoon, I remember," she continued, "and it was spring. The cactus were flowering. One of the wagons had broken a wheel. Funny that it should pick then and there to break down, on that stretch of open plain, when we had just come through what seemed an endless chain of mountains. The men were working on the wheel, and John was watching them. He was the pet of the company, my Johnnie. Sarah was picking wildflowers. I heard her scream first."

"Don't," he said, more loudly. It came from his mouth

sounding like the scrape of rusty sawteeth on metal, not at all like his voice.

"It doesn't bother me to tell it," she said, misunderstanding. Her voice was steady and cool. "It's good to tell it at last. No one ever asked me before. Not Enrique nor Soledad nor Julio. I think that they didn't want me to relive the pain. They thought they were being kind." She fingered the hem of her dress. "I suppose they were, in their way."

He cleared his throat. He didn't want to hear about murdered children. He didn't want to hear about the hell she'd been through and the ghosts that haunted her. He had enough of his own already. But there was something about the way she looked at him, and he found himself saying, "Tell it, then."

"There's not much more," she said softly. "Sarah screamed and went down in the weeds. I remember that clearly. Those red braids, there one minute, gone the next, as if the grass was a pond and she just ducked under the water. She was dead already, I suppose. The Apache had crept up all around us, you see, using those beautiful spring flowers and tall weeds for cover. I started to run toward her. Ewan grabbed me as I raced past him and swung me around. He shouted, 'The wagon, the wagon!' and 'Take John!' and thrust his spare pistol into my hands."

She stopped for a moment, staring just past Dix's shoulder. "I took John and I ran, and I threw him under the wagon with the Schumacher children and the Websters'. But I'd run to the wrong one, you see. We all had, probably because the men were there. We'd run to the wagon that only had three wheels, that was propped on a makeshift sawhorse. The last thing I remember, after I threw John beneath it, was the sound of Deborah Schumacher screaming, and that sawhorse splintering, giving way. I turned just in time to see the white of the Conestoga's canvas coming at me. I remember ducking down. And that's all."

"Your kids?" Dix heard himself ask.

"Dead," she said simply. "Everyone was dead except me. Julio and Enrique said they found me wedged beneath that half-burnt wagon. They heard me moaning. I don't remember it. They said they buried the bodies. They set my legs and my arm and hauled me back here. They were so kind to me. Soledad was so kind."

She leaned to the side and touched Soledad's arm. There was no reaction.

"So you see, I have to keep living. I *will* keep on living. For Ewan and Sarah and John, for all the people who died that day. I am their eyes and their ears. I am their breath."

Melody's thumb had fallen from her mouth. She was asleep, and Dix watched while Nancy gently eased her down onto her side and tucked a blanket about her. "Don't look so sad, Dix. You've thought of everything, and you've made us safe. Your Yancy's out there, don't forget. We'll hold off the Indians until he brings help. We will survive."

He wished he could be sure of that. He didn't know how she managed to be so calm in the face of danger, especially the danger that was coming their way. But if she was lying, her cornflower eyes didn't betray her. They were smooth as glass, calm as the halcyon seas.

He said, "Yes'm."

She broke out into a sudden grin. "That's Nancy to you, Sheriff."

"Cash, he said you make my supper?"

They both looked up, startled to find Julio standing in the shadows, just around the bend in the tunnel. He let go of Papagayo's leash, and the dog trotted between Nancy and Dix to James and licked his face. For the first time, Dix saw the boy smile.

Even if it hadn't bothered Nancy to tell him her tale, even if it had been in some way cathartic for her, it had clawed at old wounds he'd nearly forgotten he had. It might have been selfish of him, but he was glad for change in conversation. He supposed he should mosey up the tunnel and sit near the howl with Cash, but he wasn't quite ready for the barrage of wind and noise.

So, while Nancy parceled out Julio's supper and poured him his limeade, Dix leaned toward the little boy who loved the Apache enough to want to go back and live with them.

"Quite a dog you've got there," he said. "Papagayo a made-up name, or does it mean something?"

For a moment he thought the boy wasn't going to answer, but then the word came out, as ripe and round as a plum. "Parrot," James said. He kept his eyes on the panting red dog sprawled across his lap.

"Good name," said Dix. "He's sure all kinds'a colors. Blue eyes, for one thing. You don't hardly ever see a dog with blue eyes. Kind'a startlin', aren't they? Fur two shades of red, and then that copper on his legs and eyebrows. Me, I've always favored a dog with coppery eyebrows. And then that white on his face and neck."

"White feet in the back," James said. He was still looking down, staring at the dog's head.

"Forgot that part, I guess," Dix said, leaning back. "Course, I hardly saw him this morning. He sure moves like a bullet shot out of a gun. What happened to the other half of his tail?"

As if he were listening, Papagayo thumped his stubby tail on the ground and barked softly.

James shrugged. "He came that way," he said.

Dix nodded gravely. He was aware that Julio and Nancy had stopped chattering. They were both watching him and the boy.

He said, "Well, he could've had an accident, or maybe he was born that way. I've seen some cowdogs, looked something like him—some with blue eyes, too—that were born without any tail at all, or a stump no longer than your thumb."

The boy looked up at last. "Really?"

"Yup. He's sure a fine dog, whether he was born that way or not. What happened to your hand, there?"

James stared at him, and for a second, Dix thought he'd lost the boy. But then James pulled himself into a straight sit and said, "It got hurt back when they . . . a long time ago. Tábano said he had to cut them off." He raised his hand and pointed at the missing fingers. Almost defiantly, he added, "He said I was brave. He said I didn't cry. He'll come for us. You'll see."

And then he bent forward and lowered his face to rest it upon the dog's head. Signaling, Dix supposed, that the conversation was ended.

When he turned toward Nancy, tears were slowly spilling down her cheeks.

Where Yancy was, it had stopped raining. He still hadn't reached Spider Rock, which, he would kindly tell anyone who happened to ask, was a hell of a lot farther on foot than it was on horseback.

And he'd probably tell them even if they didn't ask.

He was soaking wet and chilled through, and when he pried his watch out of his pocket and flicked a match with his thumbnail, the hands read nearly eleven o'clock. He got the watch back into his pocket all right, but he dropped his match tin. After a few minutes of groping, he found it. It was open and had fallen into a puddle. All his matches were ruined.

Swearing a blue streak through chattering teeth, he wrung out his blanket—again—and went over his options.

There was still some lightning in the southern skies, but it was too far away to do him any good. The moon was little more than a sliver, and the clouds kept covering it up, along with the stars. He might try to keep limping along, but who knew where he'd limp to? With his hip hurting like blazes, he didn't want to take one more step than was necessary.

And so, finally, he just sat down and pulled his cold, wet blanket around his shoulders. He drew the last piece of jerky from his shirt pocket and ripped a piece off with his teeth.

Like it or not, he'd wait until dawn.

11

Nancy, who had at last been able to settle into a light doze, woke with a start. The lamps had been dimmed, and at first she sat very still, listening to the deep breathing of the children and Soledad's halfhearted snores. Something was different.

Thunder boomed so loudly that it seemed to shake the very walls of the tunnel. It was what had woken her, she realized.

Soledad, too, jolted awake at the crash. She sat up suddenly, startling Nancy, and twisted her head toward the mine's opening. She sniffed, scenting the air like a dog.

"Rain," she said, at the same moment that Nancy thought it.

The hum of the wind had stopped, and in its place, growing louder by the second, came the distant sound of beating raindrops falling on sun-baked soil, pounding it. Nancy reached to turn up the nearest lantern just in time to see a thin rivulet of water coming down the tunnel, following its slanted floor.

She jumped to her feet just as it reached her, and she

began shoving blankets and sleepy children out of its path. Soledad, too, leapt up. "Where are we?" she asked, her head craning to and fro like a bird's. "Has Enrique brought us into the old mine?"

"Help me," cried Nancy, and Soledad turned to the business at hand, hurriedly making a path in their belongings for the little stream, which was widening rapidly.

Thunder boomed again, so loud that it must have been right on top of them, and a flash of lightning burst so bright that for an instant it sent fingers of harsh light far back into the shaft.

Nancy called, "Help! We're drowning back here!" up the tunnel, but no one answered. She kept shifting blankets and boxes as fast as her hands could move. "This side! Over here!" she called to Soledad.

The water was rushing past now, running rapidly along the left side of the tunnel, which seemed to be the lowest. It raced past them, down into the gently sloping blackness beyond the lantern light.

The children hugged the wall, blinking and confused. Melody was shaking, and her thumb was in her mouth again. Soledad, who seemed recovered at long last, helped Nancy move baskets and boxes of food and the clock Nancy had brought, move the ammunition Dix and Julio had scoured the town for, and the spare guns and jugs of drinking water and lanterns and the quilt she'd been working on. Better the mine, she'd thought, than leave it for the Indians to burn.

"Nancy?" a confused Soledad said over the distant, but increasing, sound of beating rain. "Why are we here? Let us go to my house and build a warm fire."

The children's storybook floated away, down into the belly of the mine, down into the darkness. Melody turned her head, watched as it disappeared.

"I'll explain later," Nancy called, and rescued another

sodden blanket from the edge of the stream. Where were the men? Why hadn't they answered?

Another flash of lightning lit the shaft, and the following crash of thunder nearly startled her out of her shoes.

Just as the stream widened to cross the midway point on the dirt floor, began to tear at the edges of the haphazardly piled crates and baskets, its flow softened. As she watched, it slowly began to narrow, leaving a slick of wet clay and earth and damp gravel in its wake.

But the sound of rain, that infrequently heard but too familiar sound, hadn't ceased. The rain still came. Julio had prophesied correctly.

The men must be doing something to divert it, she realized.

Certain that their possessions were safe for at least the time being, she lifted a lantern and turned up the wick. "You children stay here, and stay out of that mud," she said.

The air had grown chilly. Soledad had been right about wanting a warm fire. She rubbed down the goose bumps on her arms and hesitated, adding, "James, you and your sister take a blanket. I'm going to go see what the men are doing."

"Send Enrique to me, Nancy," said Soledad, pulling her shawl across to cover her scarred face. She looked frightened and alone and small, very small.

For a moment, Nancy considered bringing the children along, but decided against it. Soledad seemed harmless enough at the moment, and James and Melody were already upset. That thumb in Melody's mouth was Nancy's only clue, but it was a big one. She had sucked it when she first came to Regret. She had sucked it for two days after Soledad had tried to throw her down the well. And she'd been sucking it since they came to this mine. James, stoic again after his conversation with Dix, was tucking a blanket around his sister's shoulders.

Why hadn't he told her how he'd lost those fingers? Why had he confided in Dix and not one of them? He had probably spoken more words in the last day than he had in all the months he'd been in Regret. It might have made another woman jealous to think that a stranger could elicit a response where she had tried so hard and failed, but it only left Nancy puzzled and aching for James. Aching for these poor children, who had been through so much, and were about to go through more.

"Nancy?" said Soledad, effectively jerking Nancy back to the here and now. It wasn't a long trip. "Send Enrique to me?"

Ignoring Soledad's request—how could she tell Soledad that her husband was dead, and that Soledad, herself, had been responsible?—she said, "I won't be long."

Quickly, keeping to the dry side, she scurried around the bend and up the long tunnel.

As water-soaked as three drowned eels, Dix, Cash, and Julio moved back inside the mouth of the tunnel.

"Tarnation!" Cash sputtered, blinking rapidly as the water coursed down his face. "Christ on a crutch!"

Dix leaned his shovel against the tunnel wall, then bent over and shook the water from his hair like a dog. His hat hadn't helped a bit, seeing as how Julio's enthusiasm with the pick had knocked it off in the first thirty seconds. Just about took his eye with it, too.

He looked over to see the old goatherd wringing water by the fistful from his blousy trousers and shirt.

"This storm," Julio went on with a shake of his head, "I have not seen her like for many years. All week she builds and builds. Even the little brown cockroaches hide. I knew something bad would come."

Julio leaned back against the wall and peered out the entrance, through the pelting rain. It was coming straight down in the biggest, coldest, hardest drops that Dix had ever seen, and he'd seen some whoppers. He heard Julio mutter sadly, "Poor Enrique, all of your crops are down in the field. The corn for which you worked so hard lies flat."

"Hey!" Cash yelped, water dripping from his nose as he pointed and squinted. "Hey, look, fellas! Ain't that water in the river?"

It was. A new flash of lightning illuminated the churning water. It was halfway up the banks, its surface roiled by rain. It was climbing steadily higher.

"I'll be damned," Dix whispered, rubbing at his gooseflesh. It hadn't been raining anywhere near long enough to account for that much water, no matter how fast and how hard it was coming down. The storm must be a big one. It must have been raining for quite a while to the north and to the west and up into the mountains.

Lightning, directly overhead, lit the surrounding land in a dazzling display, and he jerked involuntarily at the deafening crack of thunder. He couldn't seem to stop that. Since it had moved in so close, he'd been jerking and twitching with every boom. He comforted himself that Julio was jumpy, too, and that earlier, Cash had thrown himself over backward and right down into a puddle when a particularly big one sounded.

"Dix!"

He twisted his head toward Nancy's voice. Holding a lantern high, she stood beside the upended table. The invading water had shoved it back so that it sat on an angle in the tunnel like an open gate, with plenty of room to pass on one side. She wasn't passing, though. She shouted, "The water! It's coming again!"

"*¡Mierda!*" snapped Julio, and Dix grabbed his shovel

again. They'd been too busy marveling at the river to see what was happening right under their boots.

"Aw, crimeny," Cash said, reluctantly stepping back out into the downpour. "This ain't gonna work. We gotta dig a trench."

"Good idea!" Dix hollered. "Start diggin'!"

The rain beating at their backs, pounding their heads like a symphony of knuckles on ripe melons, they began to dig alongside the remains of the mud wall they'd built before, the wall that was rapidly melting to admit a new flood.

"This way," Julio shouted. He had the pick, and was cutting a path away from the mine shaft and down the subtle grade toward the river. It was subtle when the sun was shining, anyway. Now Dix could see the churning water sheeting, rippling past Julio.

He began to dig in earnest, following the narrow, muddy path that Julio was making. Cash was right behind him, widening the trench that Dix's shovel made. Their breath came out in clouds of vapor.

This ground was a lot easier to dig wet than dry, Dix thought, but it was sure a hell of a lot heavier.

Lightning again split the skies with an ear-shattering crack of thunder, and Dix jumped in spite of himself.

Cash stopped shoveling long enough to lift his head and shout, "Stop that, you whore!" And then he bent over double, choking on rainwater.

At last they reached Julio, who had stopped far short of the banks of the river, and they widened the end of the trench to let the water flow naturally toward its stream.

Flow, my ass, thought Dix. It was coursing, pushing near the tops of the banks now, brown, choppy water that was moving so fast that it looked to be boiling. Dix figured it had to be about fifteen feet deep and thirty across. He hoped those goats of Julio's didn't feel a sudden urge to swim to the barn.

"My goats, my poor goats," said Julio, who was apparently reading his mind. They began to work in reverse, moving back toward the mine, widening the trench, digging it deeper.

"My little goats, they hate the water," he shouted through chattering teeth as he brought the pick down again. "They do not like to be wet. I can tell you, *señor,* wherever they are at this moment, they must be very sad indeed at all this water."

"Me, too," called Cash through the torrent. "I ain't never gonna take a bath again!"

Nancy stood inside the mouth of the mine, the lantern in one hand and Papagayo's leash in the other. Soledad and the children, wrapped in blankets, had just joined her, and they all watched the men frantically digging. Nancy would have helped them, but there were no more picks, no more shovels, and she decided her hands would do little good in this downpour.

The mine had stopped flooding, at any rate. The sudden gush of water had rapidly dwindled to a trickle. When the men reached the tunnel's mouth again and widened their channel, they'd be safe, if somewhat soggy.

She thought that she had seen some real monsters of storms, but she'd never seen it come so fast and so hard. And straight down! Where had the wind gone off to? If she lived to be one hundred years old, she would never really understand Arizona weather.

"Where is Enrique?" Soledad asked. She leaned out into the storm, twisting her head from side to side. The shawl covering her head and shoulders was instantly drenched. "Why is he not helping the others?"

Hot tears suddenly pushing at the backs of her eyes,

Nancy leaned over and set the lantern down, well away from the tunnel opening's drip line. She had put it off long enough.

"Soledad . . ." she said.

"And why are we in this tunnel?" Soledad demanded. She took a step back, and steam rose from her shawl in little curls. "Enrique has told me many times that it is not safe. That is why they boarded it up so long ago! Why are we not in our houses, snug and dry?"

Gently, Nancy placed her hand on Soledad's shoulder. In Spanish, she said, "Soledad, I have some very sad news. Do you think you can take it?"

Her small, scarred face dripping, Soledad looked up. She took a breath. "Is it Enrique?"

Solemnly, Nancy nodded.

Soledad looked past her, toward the tunnel wall. "I have lost much time again," she murmured. "Too much, too much."

"Soledad," Nancy began, keeping her voice quiet and even, "this morning, two Apaches came. Enrique was killed. He died bravely, my darling. Most bravely. It happened very fast, and he did not suffer."

Soledad mouthed the word "Apache," but no sound issued from her lips. And then, just audibly, she said, "Oh, Enrique."

"We think they may be coming back." There was no sense in telling her the whole tale. Perhaps later, but not now. "That is why we have come to the mine. We have made a safe place for ourselves with food and ammunition and all our favorite things."

She didn't add that she'd brought their pet possessions—her own quilt and Soledad's mantel clock and many others—because when the Apache came, they would surely burn the town and everything in it.

"Help is coming tomorrow," she added. She prayed it wasn't a lie.

Soledad just kept staring past her shoulder, staring at nothing, saying nothing. Her face was like stone.

Quickly, Nancy glanced out into the storm. The men were roughly halfway back to the tunnel. She could hear snatches of shouted conversation over the beat and drum of the downpour. If she needed help with Soledad, they would be here soon. She rubbed at her arms. It was cold, so cold. Colder than it should be.

Returning to English again, she said, "I'm so sorry about Enrique, Soledad, so very sorry. I loved him like a dear brother."

And then Soledad looked at her, and the wildness was upon her once again. "They burn him," she said.

Nancy stepped back involuntarily, shocked that it had come so fast. "No, Soledad! There was no fire. It was a spear. That's why your side is bandaged. It got you, too. Feel it along your ribs, under your dress!"

Nancy's words fell upon deaf ears. "Apache," Soledad snarled, so softly that Nancy could barely hear her over the downpour. "They will come. They will burn us. They will burn these wild children."

Lightning flashed again, and Nancy waited for the crackling thunder to fade away before she soothed, "It's all right, Soledad," in a last ditch effort to reason with the woman. "They can't burn us here in the mine. There's nothing to burn. Dix says—"

And then Soledad shoved her out into the storm, shoved her much faster and harder than a ninety-pound woman should be able to shove. As Nancy fell backward into the beating rain and cold mud, jerking Papagayo with her, Soledad cried, "Water puts out fire! I will save these *niños,* I will save!"

Before Nancy realized what she was doing, before she

could lift a hand, Soledad had grabbed both children firmly by their arms and pulled them out into the storm, across the ditch. Dragging them behind her, she began to race through the sheeting rain toward the swollen river.

Papagayo ripped the rope leash from Nancy's hand and followed at a run, filling the air with shrill barks of warning.

12

Lightning flared.

"Stop her! Stop her! It's Soledad!"

Dix took one look at Nancy, lying in the mud and gesturing frantically out into the rain, and he dropped his shovel. Dix ran, boots slithering through hailstones and puddles and slick mud, toward Regret's momentarily lightning-bright excuse for a main street.

Soledad had a good lead on him, but she was dragging two children, and the dog was running circles around the three of them, barking and baring his teeth, trying to turn them from the river.

"If I ever call a dog dumb again, you can kick me, Lord," Dix panted as the last fingers of lightning faded. He couldn't see through the sheeting rain for more than three or four feet, but he kept running, anyway, guided by Papagayo's frenzied barks.

The rain was coming much harder now, and he ran two more steps before he realized it had turned to hail: big hail, nearly the size of a small hen's eggs. He was sorry that he'd complained to himself about the raindrops hurting, because the hail was fifty times worse. If any of them lived through this, they were going to be as spotted with bruises as a bunch of firehouse dogs.

He slipped, almost went down, and regained his balance just as the lightning came again. In that sustained flash, he saw Soledad nearing the river's edge.

The children had lost their blankets, and James was pulling backward, resisting Soledad at last. Melody went placidly along, her thumb stuck in her mouth. A chunk of hail hit her on the head and she staggered but kept walking. A barking Papagayo had planted himself between Soledad and the swollen waters, which were now creeping over the banks.

He could make it, Dix thought as he ran through the pounding hail, the breath catching painfully in his chest. If she just took them in a few feet, that would be all right, wouldn't it? They wouldn't hit the drop-off. And then he realized that even if they didn't wade out to the drop-off and suddenly plunge into water fifteen feet deep, the current in the shallows was strong. It would soon carry them off and drag them under.

They were just children, after all. They were so small. They probably couldn't swim.

The ground was white now, covered in hailstones, and he slid and slipped toward the water's edge. It was a little easier to see, what with all the white on the ground. But with every unsteady step, his curses—and his breath—rose and fogged his eyes in a cloud of vapor, obscuring his already poor vision.

He heard Cash running behind him. Or rather, he heard a thud and then a shouted, *"Damn it!"* as Cash slipped on the hailstones and went down hard.

Dix didn't turn around. He kept running.

But Soledad was quicker than both of them. When he reached the bank and the lightning flashed again, he caught a glimpse of her shawl on the bank, black against the pale hailstones. Her bobbing head and shoulders appeared for a moment as she was carried along by the swift river.

She was already out in the center of the channel, and both children were with her. Through the chop, he could make out the sodden blond of their heads moving swiftly downstream. The dog had dived in after them and paddled frantically in the current, trying in vain to snare James's collar in his teeth.

Dix was just about to dive in when Cash ran past him. "No, this way, this way!" Cash shouted over his shoulder through the pelt of hail. "Downstream!"

Ignoring his aching lungs and his bombarded scalp, Dix ran, slipping and sliding, after Cash.

Nancy slid through the hailstones after them. They felt and sounded like marbles, a million misshapen marbles under her feet and pounding her scalp, her face, her body, and more falling all the time.

Julio was in front of her, but not so far as Cash and Dix. Julio's white shirt and pants made him the only one visible through the storm, and she followed blindly, tripping and stumbling, falling many times but always scrambling to her feet again.

The hail, which had started out the size of small, new apples—and every bit as hard—was rapidly dwindling to a bean-sized spatter. But it was still coming thickly, and it was still slick. Hailstones had adhered to her hems in soggy clusters, and her skirts felt as if they weighed a hundred pounds. But she barely gave this a thought, except to curse it for slowing her progress. All she knew was that the children and Soledad had gone into the waters of that muddy, roiling river.

She saw Julio pause, then stop, then start running again. *Please, dear God,* she prayed silently as she ran, gasping for breath, *please save them. Please help Dix get to them in time.*

Cash ran past the bobbing, sputtering heads, and Dix was on his heels. He figured that Cash's plan was to get far enough in front of them that he'd have time to swim out across the current and intercept them. It seemed as good a strategy as any. That was, if they hadn't already drowned by then.

He was going to get those kids out of there, and he was by God going to save Papagayo, too. That was a damn fine dog.

And when he got Soledad out, he was going to tie her up and put her safely out of the way for the duration, no matter what Nancy said.

He reached the bank just as Cash ripped off his boots and dived in. He followed suit and was in the water only a second later.

The water came as a shock. The air had been cold, but this water was icy, so icy that for a moment it paralyzed him. Then he saw Cash, stroking through the muddy chop, heading for midstream. Dix kicked hard, straight up, and managed to raise his shoulders from the water for just a moment.

It was long enough. He spotted Melody's blond head, coming for a point only ten feet from where he struggled.

He swam like the devil himself was after him, and with every stroke, every mouthful of muddy water that he spat out just in time to take in a new one, he thanked his daddy for tossing him in Kirby Creek when he was six.

The current fought him, but he pushed on. The water threw things at him, battered him with sticks and chunks of cactus and limbs of trees it had collected miles away. All were caught up in its wild current.

He couldn't see Melody, couldn't see anything but the

muddy water in his eyes and the hail pelting him from above and floating on the water that roiled all around him. He swam blindly, battered by stray branches, mindlessly headed for that point where he hoped his and Melody's paths would converge.

The current carried him farther downriver, but he always pulled for the center. And every time his mouth wasn't full of floodwater or hail or twigs, he shouted, "Melody! James! Soledad!"

And then something hit him from the side again, this time something soft and small. He latched onto it and found it was Melody.

She hadn't lost consciousness, thank God. Her eyes were wide and teary, her golden hair in muddy strings. Coughing, she grabbed hold of his neck like she'd never let go.

Fighting to keep his head out of the water, he began to stroke back toward the bank, shielding her tiny form with his body and rearranging her grasping hands so that he could breathe again. And as he did, he became aware that she was making a sound, a tiny, high-pitched keen, a thin wail that cut through the noise of the water's rush and roar like a blade. And then one tiny word, a tearful, wailed prayer.

"Daddy!"

"It's all right, baby," he said hoarsely, hugging her closer while he fought the current like a man possessed. "You're safe. Daddy's here."

He said it to Melody, and he said it to Clara. Poor Clara, who he'd come too late to save.

"Daddy's here."

Julio was ahead, pacing Cash, and Nancy ran down the bank, keeping even with Dix. All the hail on the ground made it easier to see, even when there was no lightning, and Julio's white pants and shirt stood out like a beacon as he traveled the bank. Not that Nancy was watching him at the moment.

When she'd first seen Melody in Dix's arms, both her hands had come up to her mouth, and she'd begun to sob. And when Dix pulled Melody's tiny body to shore, still breathing, still clinging to his neck, Nancy nearly broke down.

But she didn't. She slipped and slid her way to meet them. They rose from the rushing waters in a cloud of steamy vapor, and Dix carried the girl to her, saying softly, "You're all right, Melody. You're all right, baby. Let go, now."

Miraculously, Melody seemed to hear him and obeyed, twisting in his arms to fold her hands on either side of Nancy's neck.

Nancy looked at her in amazement. She smoothed the girl's cold brow with her fingers and then took her from Dix. Instead of hanging like a rag doll, Melody ringed Nancy's neck with her arms and hung on hard. Against her ear, Melody murmured, "Mama, Mama," and then began to cry softly.

"Thank you, God," whispered Nancy. Cradling the little girl, lost no more, she sank slowly to her knees upon the white hailstones, tears coursing down her cheeks. "Thank you."

Dix ran along the riverbank, wishing he'd remembered to bring his damn boots. Ahead, he saw the blurry white shape that could only be Julio trotting quickly along the bank. Then he got close enough to see Cash, backstroking to beat the band and headed for the bank on an angle. James's collar was in his fist, and James was alive. He was kicking, too, his small feet making a froth on the water's choppy surface.

Nancy was right. Cash was a good boy, underneath. A good man.

But Dix couldn't see Soledad or the dog anywhere. He ran past Julio, calling, "Soledad! Papagayo!" over and over. And then the lightning flashed, farther away than it had been before, and he saw just a hint of black fabric, just the hem of a skirt, before it was pulled down beneath the current. He ran on, searching the chop for any sign, but he didn't see it again.

At last he stopped running and bent over, hands on his knees. "Soledad," he whispered between ragged breaths. "I'm sorry, Soledad. I can't . . . can't run anymore."

The dog was nowhere to be seen. Perhaps, lacking the children, he'd finally latched hold of her and pulled her down, just to make her stop.

Soaked through, bruised, freezing, and weary to the bone, he slumped down on the melting hail. It had stopped hailing, he realized. He didn't know when. The night was too cold and still overcast in spots, but the air was clear. There wasn't even a hint of a breeze. The rushing river, dry this afternoon, probably dry for years, made the only sounds in the night.

That, and Julio's approaching footsteps.

"*¿Qué tal, señor?*" the old man asked quietly.

Dix didn't look up. "Just bury me here, Julio," he said. It was a crying shame about Soledad. She was as crazy as a bedbug, but he wished he could have saved her. He wished he could have saved that dog.

"The little girl, she is all right?"

Dix nodded. He was still out of breath. "Cash and the boy," he said with difficulty. "They get to shore safely?"

"*Sí.*"

"Soledad went under before I could get to her," Dix panted. He stared at the melting hailstones between his cold, stockinged feet. "I followed. Didn't see her again."

He felt Julio's hand touch his shoulder. Gently, he said, "It is God's will. You understand, I do not mean any disrespect. But for a long time, she has wished to be dead. I think, in her heart, she died a long time ago. She is with Enrique, now. She is at peace."

Dix looked out across the river. The far bank was as white as the one he was sitting on. "Sorry about Papagayo."

Sadly, the old man said, "I think those thankless goats will not miss him at all. But I will. And the boy will, most of all. He was a fine dog. He deserved a rich house to live in and guard, and many sheep or cattle to herd. He would have liked that. We could not offer him much, only my poor goats."

Every bone and muscle in his body complaining, Dix slowly got to his feet. He didn't relish the walk back up the bank to where he'd left his boots. They'd come so far downriver that he couldn't see the blasted town, even when the lightning flashed. Only the thought that he'd managed to save that little button of a girl, that she'd called him Daddy, gave him the strength to move.

Daddy.

Julio walking slowly beside him, Dix started to doggedly put one foot in front of the other. He wanted to get back and get dry and have a long, satisfying look at that little girl. Maybe she didn't remember calling him that or hugging him for dear life, but he'd remember it until he died.

But before he'd taken three steps, Julio jutted his arm out, stopping him cold. "You hear that, *señor?*"

"What?"

Julio shushed him and listened hard. Dix didn't hear a blamed thing, but suddenly Julio joyously cried, *"Ay, Dios mío!"* and trotted back the other way.

Dix didn't much fancy walking on hailstones in his

stockinged feet any farther than was absolutely necessary, so he stood and watched as the old man jogged back down the bank.

About fifty feet past the place where Dix had crumpled to the ground, exhausted, Julio stopped and stooped at the water's edge. He lifted something from the shallows, something that Dix couldn't make out until the next flash of lightning. It looked for all the world like a limp and dripping gunnysack, half filled with grain and steaming to beat the band.

But it wasn't a sack, Dix realized as Julio walked nearer, hugging it to his chest.

Gunnysacks didn't have four legs, a head, and half a weakly wagging tail.

"Papagayo," Dix whispered to himself, momentarily forgetting how cold he was and how wet and how sore. "Good boy, Papagayo."

13

"I don't care if those Apaches come down on us right this instant," Nancy said firmly. "These children need dry clothing. I could say the same for the both of you."

They were all gathered in the front room of Nancy's adobe. Hail had fanned in a little way through the open front door and was currently melting into the packed dirt floor. But compared to the damage the windstorm had done, the hail was nothing.

By the light of the dying fire, Dix could see that the floor was covered in debris and that two of the checkered curtains that draped the cupboards had been blown clean off, doweling and all.

The chairs had been blown over, too, and one lay in pieces against the far wall. She had righted two of them, though, and had seated the children, dressed in dry but obviously outgrown clothes, while she ruffled their wet hair with what looked like an old flour sack.

"Well, don't just stand there, you fellows," she said, all business. "I believe Enrique had some clothes that would fit you, Dix. Cash is already over there." And then her eye lit on the bundle Julio carried, and her face softened. "Oh, Julio! You found the wee bonny thing!"

In a flash, she whisked Papagayo out of Julio's arms and carried him to the fire. She laid him gently on the hearth. He raised his head and licked her hand, his tail thumping the adobe bricks.

"About Soledad . . ." Dix began.

"I know," she said thickly, and he couldn't see her face. "Cash told me. Now, get going," she said, all business again. She stood up and smoothed her apron. "There are still clouds moving this way. The storm could come up again any time now."

Puzzled but too tired to argue, Dix gestured to Julio, and the two men started up the street, over the melting and all but vanished hail, to Enrique's and Soledad's little house. At least he had his boots back, he thought. He'd be damned if he knew what had happened to his hat.

The river was already receding. From what little he could tell in the gloom, it was still moving fast but, miraculously, it had narrowed its channel. It now ran about a foot below the level of its rocky banks. It had topped them and spread wide just minutes before.

And how did Cash know about Soledad, anyway?

Julio left him in front of Enrique's house. "I go to the barn," he explained. "I have my things there, and a change of clothing." A small smile crooked the corner of his mouth. "I also have some whiskey."

Dix remembered the state Julio had been in when he and Cash and Yancy first battled their way into town—had it been only twenty-four hours ago?—and said, "Just don't get so sozzled you can't shoot, *amigo.*"

Julio's smile broadened. *"Sí, patrón,"* he said and, throwing Dix a wink, went on his way.

Dix opened the door and went in. Unlike Nancy's place, this one had been shut up tight and hadn't suffered the worst effects of the storm. Six crude chairs still stood in a loose circle, ringing the place where the table had been until they'd hauled it to the mine, and a flickering votive candle sat on the seat of one of them. He could hear Cash knocking around in the back room.

"Cash?" he called, glancing about him. This house was just like Nancy's in layout, but not in detail. A picture of a Mexican marketplace, colorfully if crudely painted, was hung over the mantel. Bright Mexican blankets were tossed over the rocking chairs flanking the fireplace, and there was a small altar against the back wall. Probably where Cash had swiped the candle from, Dix thought.

A three-legged table sat beneath one of the front windows. There was a flowerpot on it that held a little cactus, and a few pieces of pretty crockery. He hadn't paid any attention while they were moving the big table out.

You wouldn't have known to look at it that a crazy woman lived here. Or a brave but foolish man.

Cash appeared in the rear doorway, holding another votive candle. "Nothin' fits," he said sourly. There was a cloth wound round his head, a cloth dampened by the stain of blood. Enrique's baggy, white pants just skimmed his boot tops, and the shirt stopped halfway to his wrists.

"You leave anything for me?" Dix asked, trying not to smile. It wasn't that difficult. He hardly had the energy to talk.

"Yeah," Cash said, coming forward into the front room. "There's a few things left, I guess." He sagged into a chair. "What time is it, anyway? My watch got drowned."

Dix dug into his pocket and, after some peering and shaking, he said, "Mine, too."

"They'll dry out."

Dix wasn't so sure. He said, "Live in hope." He'd got a watch wet about sixteen years ago wading the Big Sandy

Creek after Renny Foster and some stolen cattle, and it hadn't dried out yet. Well, it had, but it hadn't started working again.

He asked, "What happened to your head?"

Cash's hand went to the cloth bandage. "One'a them big balls'a hail cut it, I guess. Sure got thumped by a bunch of 'em. Never seen nothin' like it! Hail, sure, but not that big and mean. Nancy—Mrs. MacGregor, I mean—said I was bleedin' somethin' fierce. She fixed it up for me. She's real nice."

"Suppose she is, when nobody's pointin' a gun at her."

Cash made a face. "How many times I gotta say I'm sorry?"

Dix didn't answer. He picked up the candle from the chair and went back through the doorway Cash had just come from.

Behind the main one, there were two small rooms, hardly bigger than cells, which opened off a very short hall. To the left, he found a workroom, crammed with jars of preserves and baskets of fabric scraps piled on a dusty loom. A cobwebbed spinning wheel sat in one corner.

He backed up and went into the tiny bedroom, and soon found a decent pair of trousers and a shirt. They were a fair fit, if a little tight across the chest. It felt uncommonly good to get out of his wet clothes, and it took quite a bit of willpower to keep from just crawling onto that bed and going straight to sleep.

His wet clothes held away from his body as he carried Enrique's spare hat, he rejoined Cash in the main room. Cash must have been beat out, too. His head was on his chest, the candle was about to drop from his fingers, and he was dozing off.

"Wake up," said Dix.

Cash's head jerked up and his eyes blinked rapidly. "Wasn't asleep," he said hoarsely.

"Sure, you weren't," Dix said. He sat down in the rocker next to Cash and leaned forward, propping his elbows on his knees. "I wanted to tell you that you did a fine thing tonight, son, pullin' that boy out of the water."

Cash shrugged. He stared into the cold fireplace. "Wasn't nothin' you didn't do, Sheriff. I guess anybody would have tried. Sure wish I could'a got that crazy Mex lady out, though."

"I couldn't save her, either," Dix said softly.

Cash snorted. "Don't know how you could've. She was dead when I grabbed her. Almost lost the kid, too. That blamed dog had hold of his collar and wouldn't leave go for nothin'! Couldn't pull the two of 'em to shore, so I had to punch the dog in the head to get him to turn loose."

A flush of anger suddenly heated Dix's veins, and he turned toward Cash.

But Cash wasn't looking. "Sure hope that dog got out okay. Damned if he didn't take a chunk of the kid's shirt with him. He wasn't turnin' loose for love nor money." Cash rocked back in his chair. "Sure like to have me a dog like that. You see the way he was paddlin' after them? Lord a'mighty!"

The anger had backed off a little, but Dix said, "You punched him? In the head?"

Cash turned toward him at last. "Well, sure! It was either that, or all three of us was goin' to heaven. Figured you'd rather have that kid alive than three corpses to bury. And one less feller to help shoot back come mornin'."

Dix stood up, his knees complaining loudly. "Julio found the dog," he said. Cash had done the right thing, after all. He didn't like the idea of slugging a dog much at all, but he supposed he would have done it himself, if push came to shove. "Papagayo made it to shore downstream."

Cash rose, too, and picked up his dripping pile of clothing. "I'm right glad to hear that," he said. "Right glad." And then he lifted his candle higher, looking Dix up and down.

"Sheriff?" he asked. "You play anything? Banjo? A guitar or a harmonica or some such?"

Puzzled, Dix said, "Why?"

"'Cause we could sure as shootin' get ourselves a job as a mariachi band, rigged out like this."

Dix grinned and slapped Cash on the back. "Guess we could at that," he said. "Let's get back to the mine."

Nancy dozed fitfully, sinking down into a welcome sleep, and each time rising from it in a small panic.

The children were asleep on her right, bundled under blankets in their cast-off clothing. That afternoon, she'd brought everything that fit them to the mine, and she didn't have the heart to make them change again. Besides, every other stitch they owned was probably soaked through. The second flood through the tunnel had been wider, if briefer.

She'd changed, too, once they got back to the mine, but she thought she'd never be warm again. The dress she presently wore had sustained the least water damage, being soaked only on the skirts. She'd gotten the worst of it wrung out. But she was still huddled in two thin wool blankets that failed to entirely hold back the chill of the night.

She glanced at Soledad's clock. Two-fifteen. Another three hours or so, and it would be light. She had to get some sleep.

The men were all up near the mouth of the shaft, having pushed the table around to block it again. Likely one was awake and standing guard while the others slept.

She hoped they were sleeping more soundly than she was.

Papagayo, who was nestled on a blanket to her left,

stretched in his sleep and turned over on his back, his front paws in the air, the damp feathers hanging down in careless knots. He hummed and groaned contentedly.

"You take forever to dry, you dear, silly thing," she whispered kindly, and tucked his blanket about him again. "Remind me to give you a good brushing."

Someone whispered, "You awake?"

It was Dix, just coming down the tunnel. He looked strange in Enrique's clothing. She had never before seen those trousers circled by a gun belt.

"Barely," she whispered in reply. "And why aren't you sleeping?"

He sat down on his heels, carefully avoiding the worst of the mud. The tunnel smelled dank and mildewy, and the air was thick with cold humidity. It would be a good deal worse when the sun came up, she knew.

She also knew that by afternoon, this tunnel would be an oven. Oh, it would be cooler than outside, maybe twenty degrees cooler. But when it was a hundred and ten degrees above and ninety degrees in here, when there was no freshening breeze, only the closeness of six trapped bodies . . .

"Dozed for a couple hours, I guess," Dix said, jerking her thoughts back.

Really, he was a fine-looking man, wasn't he? Perhaps not exactly handsome. No, not handsome, you couldn't call him that. Rugged, that was it, she decided. And comforting, somehow. Despite everything, despite the flood and the storm and the threat that the dawn would bring, he made her feel safer.

Softly, he said, "Cash is standing guard duty. Julio's out like a light."

"He found his jug, I take it?" she said with a faint smile.
Dix nodded. "Just enough for medicinal purposes.

Could'a used a nip myself. Said he wants to prove his marksmanship tomorrow."

"He was a sharpshooter, you know. In the Mexican War. And why didn't you? Have a nip, I mean."

He grinned sheepishly. "There wasn't any left. And no, I guess I didn't know that about him."

He reached over and moved the dog's blanket aside for a moment, resting his hand briefly on Papagayo's flanks and belly. The dog looked up with slitted blue eyes, then closed them again. "Still wet," he said with a bemused shake of his head. He looked over at Melody, letting his gaze linger gently. "Kids okay?"

Nancy nodded. "Yes, thank God. Better than okay." How could she tell him that it had made her heart burst when Melody spoke to her? That he had saved the child in more ways than he could know? She said, "I can't thank you enough."

Dix sat back again, rocking on his heels, and stared at his hands. "Wish we could have got to Soledad in time."

"I said a prayer for her. I think she wanted it this way, the poor wee lass."

Dix looked up. "Where'd you come from?"

The question took her by surprise, and it was a moment before she said, "Pittsburgh."

"Always?"

"Oh. Glasgow. But I was very small. We sailed for America when I was five."

He nodded, as if this solved some great dilemma for him, and she studied his face. His eyes were deep blue. No, deep blue gray, like an Atlantic sky just before the dawn. Funny that she hadn't noticed before. She had only noticed that they were kind eyes, good eyes.

She said, "Why do you ask?"

"Just couldn't figure you, that's all," he said. "You've got just a touch of the brogue on your tongue. I couldn't tell if it was Scots or Irish. I'm no good telling accents, that's all."

She sat, waiting for him to go on.

"It's mostly when you get excited, or when you're talkin' about the people you care about. Like Soledad. Or the kids." He shrugged. "I just wondered, that was all."

"We were both from Scotland," she said. "Ewan was from Ayr, on the Firth of Clyde."

He looked at her oddly, and she added, "A firth's a finger of the sea, sticking into the land. A little like a bay. My parents picked Ewan for me when I was seventeen. He was quite a bit older than I, but they said the match would keep the blood of the highlands pure in our children. He built houses in Pittsburgh, but he'd been a fisherman back home, in Ayr. Imagine a fisherman, out here in all this desert. Well, I suppose he would've been in his element tonight."

She smiled and shook her head. "I learned to love him, in time. He was a dreamer, my Ewan. In California, he said, all the fish would be fat and the waters warm, and there'd be no winter to freeze the nets as they came out of the sea. I wasn't so whimsical. I made him contact an agent and buy land with my dowry money, just in case the fishing was poor. I have three hundred and sixty acres near somewhere called Los Angeles."

All this talk of lost husbands, or perhaps the sea, seemed to unsettle Dix, and she felt sorry for it. He said, "Is that where you're going after this?"

She hadn't really thought about anything after the coming day. In fact, she hadn't remembered the land until just this minute, hadn't given it a thought in all this time.

Dix was right, of course. They couldn't stay in Regret, not even if Enrique and Soledad had lived. For her, this place would be marked forever with kindness, but also with blood.

She said, "I suppose. I don't know. That land'd take a man's hand, I'm afraid. Perhaps I'll sell it. We'll find a place, the children and I."

Dix stood up. "I'm right sorry about your husband, Nancy. About all your family. I mean that."

"It's past," she said simply. "Life goes where it will and drags us along."

"I reckon," he said.

"Where are you from, Dix?" she asked. She wasn't just making conversation. She really wanted to know, suddenly wanted him to tell her about his childhood and his parents and what he had done with his life before he came here. She wanted to know all about him.

What made this man, this stranger, risk his very life to help people he didn't know? She knew that he wore a badge, but Regret was far from his jurisdiction. He didn't owe them anything. He could have ridden out this morning with Yancy. Even slowed down by Cash, on foot, they would have been far away from Regret when the first of the Indians came poking around.

"Gushing Rain," he said, peering at her like she'd lost her mind.

She scowled at him teasingly. "I mean originally." Hardly a soul under the age of consent was from here. It was too new a place.

"New Mexico, mostly," he said, and before she could ask another question, he had turned and walked back up the tunnel.

"Odd," she whispered, once he had rounded the turn. "Such a fine man, though, isn't he, Papagayo?"

In his sleep, the dog hummed.

She took it for a yes.

14

Dix felt the thickness in the air along with the first gray orange fingers of the dawn. It had been the change in the air, the feeling of breathing something alien and heavy, that woke him. He was surprised that he had nodded off again when he'd been so sure that he couldn't.

"Just the trickle," said Julio's disembodied voice.

For just a second Dix thought he was hearing things, but when he creakily got to his feet, he saw the old man. He was on the other side of the overturned table, a black silhouette against the tunnel's mouth. He sat quietly, his rifle across his knees.

"What?" Dix said, and he sidled slowly around the edge of their makeshift blind. Lately, he found it didn't pay to get up, especially when he'd been sleeping on the ground. All his parts woke up at different times, and in different stages of hurt. Pressing a hand to the small of his back, he stepped over Cash's sleeping form and joined Julio at the mine's entrance.

Julio pointed. "The river."

It was, indeed, just a trickle. It looked like there was

barely a foot of water lapping lazily at the bottom of the rocky bed. The only clues to last night's fury were the big, broken limbs from trees that had grown miles and miles away, limbs that had been tossed casually along its bottom and thrown up here and there along its banks, as if by the hand of a giant.

He heard birds singing and saw the chickens pecking the mud around the barn. He spied one lonely nanny goat, foraging through what was left of the cornfield, working her way toward the flattened hay.

Julio stood up and stretched. "There will be fish," he said. "Big ones. They wash down from somewhere above, somewhere that has water all the time, where the river does not flow underground." Sweat was already beginning to bead on his brow and trickle down his nose. He held his rifle out to Dix. "It has been many years since I have had a nice, fresh fish. I go get us some breakfast. You cover me, just in case?"

But Dix pushed the gun back at him. "Not this morning, Julio." He scanned the distance, squinting. "Just because you can't see 'em yet doesn't mean they aren't out there."

Julio shrugged, and Dix added, "'Sides, I don't cotton to eatin' my fish raw, and there's no way I'm gonna advertise by building a fire."

Julio sighed and said, *"Sí, es verdad.* Some fresh fish would have been nice for breakfast, though. It would have been good with those fried corn tortillas that Nancy brought." He sat down again and mopped his brow. "The day will be steamy, *señor."*

Dix scowled and grunted his agreement. He hoped the weather was all they'd have to worry about. He hoped Yancy had made it back up to Gushing Rain. That help was already on its way.

But who was he fooling? He could count the men on one hand who'd happily ride off to fight the Apache without a gun to their heads. He should have sent Yancy east, to Fort Lowell, or west, to Fort Yuma. But both forts were over a hundred miles away. If he'd sent Yancy to either one, it'd be nearly half a week before the troops reached them.

Even under the best of circumstances, they couldn't hold out that long.

He put his back against the dirt wall of the mine and slowly slid down to sit on his heels. It was a hell of a spot they were in, all right. Maybe he should have tried to get everybody out on foot yesterday morning. Maybe they could have found a place to hole up, back in that canyon.

Maybe Enrique and Soledad would still be alive, and he wouldn't be wearing a dead man's clothes.

"It is good, what you have done," Julio said, and Dix looked up abruptly. "Sending the goats to wander, I mean," the old man said thoughtfully. "I think they will be safer. They hate the rain, but maybe it washes some of the stink off my Matamoros."

"Matamoros?"

Julio held fingers to his head, making horns. "My he goat. He smells bad. Smells like a he goat." He smiled, his wrinkles fanning wide. "He makes good goat babies, though. More males than females. I cut the males and make wethers of them, and when they are grown, they give us much good meat. I do not like to butcher the lady goats."

Julio would have gone on speaking, but something had caught Dix's eye on the other side of the river, and he signaled for silence. Intently, both men searched the land beyond the far bank, craning their heads for several moments before Dix saw a blurry dot of familiar color. He relaxed and sagged back on his heels.

"Coyote," he whispered. It slunk briefly from the distant brush before it disappeared again.

But Julio shook his head. He pointed up, toward the shaft's ceiling, and carefully scooted back until he was well inside its shadowy mouth.

Dix heard it, then. Just a faint scuffing. The sound of vegetation being brushed by careful feet. He hoped it was a goat, but he, too, moved stealthily back into the tunnel. With Julio, he slipped back behind the table barricade.

A spattering of pebbles and dust fell down over the opening, clattering softly into the light inches beyond the entrance.

Dix covered the sleeping Cash's mouth with his hand to keep him silent. Cash woke at once, and glanced angrily at Dix before he appeared to realize the situation. He nodded curtly, and Dix let go.

Dix hoped Nancy was awake. He hoped she knew to keep the dog quiet. Maybe they'd get out of this yet. Maybe the Apaches wouldn't think to look in the mine. Maybe, after they'd gone through the town and taken what they wanted and burned the rest, they'd just go on their way.

Too many maybes.

But the longer they could put off being discovered, the better.

All three men hunched shoulder to shoulder behind the shield of Soledad's tabletop. Three pairs of eyes watched the entrance. Three gun barrels were leveled and at the ready.

Another small spray of dirt rained down, clattered at the entrance.

Dix felt Cash tensing beside him. "Easy, son," he mouthed.

Suddenly, a single brave jumped down, landing in a

squat right outside the opening and startling them all. His back was turned toward them.

Dix signaled the others to wait.

The brave stood up into a crouch and gestured to the side, signaling to another brave. Or six, or twenty. Dix had no way of knowing. He found he was holding his breath, and he forced himself to breath shallowly, soundlessly. Sweat ran into his eyes, but he didn't blink. He didn't take his eyes off that brave.

And then the Apache moved away from the mine, slinking slowly and soundlessly toward the little adobes, avoiding the boards blown from the ruined frame dwellings. Two more joined him from the left, then three. By the time he got down past the cemetery to the remains of the first wooden building, there were nine braves that Dix could see. Probably twice as many that he couldn't.

"Aw, shit," breathed Cash.

"*Sí,*" whispered Julio grimly. "*Mierda.*"

Yancy was dreaming that he was at home, a kid again, and his ma was trying to roust him out of bed.

"Aw, quit it, Ma!" he muttered in his sleep.

But she kept on poking, and he was about to tell her that it was Saturday, for cripes sake, and Tyrone's turn to milk old Flossie, and didn't she know that?

And then he realized with a start that his bedroom had got all brown, and then that he was wrapped under a blanket, and that the blanket was wet, and that somebody was poking him through it.

"Hey!" he shouted, and tore the blanket away. It took him a bit longer than he'd anticipated. "You from Gushing Rain?" he asked, still fighting the last fold. "I need—"

He stopped right there and swallowed hard. What had been poking him was a rifle barrel, and it was in the hand of a grinning Mexican. The man was afoot, and behind

him, seven more Mexicans, draped in gun belts that criss-
crossed their chests, sat their lean horses. They wore
smiles that were way too friendly.

Bandidos.

"Great," Yancy muttered beneath his breath. *Just perfect.*

"Buenos días, señor," said the one who had poked him.
He broadened his smile, exposing a wide gap where his
two front teeth should have been.

"Howdy, yourself," Yancy answered, quickly looking
over the group. He knew who these boys were, all right.
He'd known the moment he saw them. He had paper on
them back in town. He took slight comfort in the fact that
the Alba gang didn't have a reputation for killing people.
At least, not many.

Still, he could have thought of a very long list of folks
he'd rather have run into this morning.

No one answered him, and he added, "Nice mornin'."
Sweat trickled down his collar. The one with no front
teeth slid Yancy's pistol from its holster—with no resistance from Yancy—and twirled it high for the others to
see. He'd already taken Yancy's Winchester. The man on
the end of the line held it proudly, the butt against his
thigh.

"A little muggy for my taste," said the man in the middle
of the mounted line.

It was Juan Alba himself. He was as distinct as the
picture on his wanted poster: slender and tall and quite
handsome, with a big but neatly trimmed mustache and
sharp, black, intelligent eyes. Yancy thought that if he'd
met Alba on the street—and if he hadn't seen the paper
on him—he'd have never figured him for the man who
had cleaned out the banks at San Xavier and Mesquite.
Among others. The Alba gang raided both sides of the

border, but Yancy was surprised to see them so far north of it.

Alba folded his long hands on his saddle horn and leaned forward slightly, bending his elbows. "Why are you out on the desert all alone, wrapped in a blanket and looking like a big brown rock, Deputy?"

His heart sank at the word. His badge. Yancy closed his eyes for a second, trying to will away the panic. The damn badge had ended all questions. They'd kill him for certain, now.

Willing his voice to stay even, which it didn't, he said, "Horse lamed himself up a few miles back. Been caught out in the storm all night. Don't suppose you fellas're headed toward Gushing Rain, are you?"

Well, he'd tried, he thought dismally. The men seemed to think he'd made a joke, because a chuckle went across the line of riders.

"Sorry, *Señor* Deputy," said Alba. "Gushing Rain is not on our itinerary at the moment."

The man next to him, a particularly nasty fellow who looked like he'd shoot his mama for a three-cent nickel, then sell her to a soap factory, laughed and said, "Itinerary? That is a good word, Juanito!"

Alba ignored him. He pointed at Yancy's chest. "I have always wanted a badge like that for my own."

Yancy just stood there. Toothless grabbed him by the shirt and ripped his badge off before he knew what was happening. The badge, with a little scrap of Yancy's shirt still clinging to it, was tossed to Alba.

Alba bent it easily with his fingers. "Tin!" he announced in disappointment, but he straightened it and pinned it to his chest anyway. His comrades seemed to admire the effect.

He pointed to Yancy's boots. "I like those, too," he said.

All Yancy could think to say was, "They're wet."

"They will dry," said Alba. "I would like them, if you please."

When Yancy hesitated, Alba's smile faded. He said, "This was not a request." He gestured to Toothless.

Toothless rammed the butt of his rifle into Yancy's side, right into the place Nancy MacGregor had bandaged two short nights before. With a grimace, Yancy fell, gripping his belly. He landed with a groan, smack in a mud puddle and right on his bad hip. From the sound of it, the bandits thought this was pretty goddamned hilarious.

Yancy didn't glance up at them, though. He was busy skinning off those boots and trying to think what he should do.

He hadn't come up with anything by the time he'd finished, so he handed the boots to Toothless, who in turn handed them up to Alba. Alba held them out at arms' length, studying them thoughtfully.

Yancy didn't get up, but he felt his side. His hand came away bloody. What would they do next? Drag him through the cactus until he was dead? Stake him out and leave him for the buzzards?

He'd never had to tangle with a Mexican gang while he'd been working for Dix, but he'd heard plenty of stories. They could think up some downright grisly things to do to a man, almost as bad as an Apache.

Maybe worse.

He hoped with all his heart that they'd just shoot him.

Alba finished his inspection and said, "You have big feet, Deputy." He dropped the boots. The Mexicans laughed.

And this careless gesture jerked Yancy straight out of good and scared and sent him directly to good and mad. It wasn't enough that these fellas had to kill you. No, they had to take your badge and your boots and make fun of your feet before they did it!

His hip was aching, his side was on fire, and his arm wasn't in such great shape, either, but he struggled to his feet. He shoved a surprised Toothless out of the way with his good arm.

"Fine," he spat. "Go ahead and make fun'a me. Go ahead and shoot me. But before you do, you oughta know why I'm out here."

Alba swept his hand to the side in a grand gesture. "Speak, *señor.*"

"I'm headed back to Gushing Rain to get help, that's all," Yancy said angrily, doing his best to ignore their chuckling. "There's some people down in a little ghost town called Regret that need help in a real big hurry. Just six of 'em, and half are Mexicans, in case you're interested. Enrique and Soledad—can't remember their last name—and this old goatherd named Julio, and a lady named Nancy, and two little kids. I'm tellin' you 'cause somebody oughta know their names. Somebody oughta remember them."

He took a quick gulp of air. "Me and Sheriff Dix Granger had us ahold of a prisoner a couple nights back, and the storm pushed us into Regret. But Soledad, she shot an Apache 'cause . . . well, 'cause she's crazy, I guess."

Alba cocked a brow.

"It's pretty goddamned complicated, all right?" Yancy snapped. "But they're holed up down there with the whole of the Apache nation comin' down on their heads, and I'm ridin' to bring help—which likely won't be much help even if I bring it—except my damn horse stepped in a chuckhole, and now you boys are about to drag me through the cactus with no boots."

He stopped, panting. He'd known when he started that

it wasn't going to do a damn bit of good, but he had to say it.

Alba scowled at him.

"I just thought you oughta know," said Yancy defiantly, scowling right back. "That's all. You can go ahead and shoot me now."

He balled his hands into fists and waited.

15

"**What are they** doin'?" Cash hissed.

Several more Indians, stripped and greased for battle, had appeared from the low weeds and scrub to the north. Dix counted fifteen, now. He figured they'd left their ponies staked out a ways, then crept in.

"They'll check the houses first," he whispered, then held his finger over his lips, silencing any further discussion.

Julio tapped him on the shoulder and pointed up at the ceiling.

That same sound, the whisk and grab of thorny brush against soft leather boots. As one, all three men held their breath.

And then came the sound that Dix had dreaded: a low growl, magnified by the tunnel walls. Swearing, he turned his head. But the drum of paws grew rapidly nearer, along with the sudden explosion of frenzied barking. It was in Dix's ear by the time he wheeled. He caught Papagayo in midair, just before the dog sailed over the table.

While he struggled to control the snarling, barking dog,

who proved harder to hang onto than a greased shoat in his twisted position, he heard half a whoop, and then gunfire exploded next to his ear, cutting it off sharply.

Things happened very quickly then, things that seemed to have no order. Nancy suddenly appeared, pulling the thrashing dog from his arms. Cash was firing—and Julio, too—and by the time he turned around again, a spear had pierced the tabletop, its point stopping less than an inch from his belly.

Two bodies lay just outside the tunnel's mouth. It was quiet again.

"God*damn!*" said Cash, his eyes wide. Nervously, he wiped his brow on his sleeve. "Jesus Christ almighty! You should'a let that damn dog drown, Julio. Daddy al'ays said as how blue-eyed dogs was bad luck!"

Never taking his eyes from the glare at the tunnel's mouth, Julio said calmly, "My papa, he always said the same about Anglo boys with guns. But I have let you live, have I not?"

"Hold on a consarned minute!" Cash said angrily, just as a single arrow whooshed through the tunnel and knocked Julio's hat from his head. It flew back into the darkness.

"Shut up, kid," Dix hissed, scanning the distance. He could see neither hide nor hair of the shooter. As far back from the mouth as they were, his range of vision was narrowed considerably. It was like looking through a telescope with the lens busted out. In addition, the morning sun was blasting him straight in the eyes.

"I liked that hat," mumbled Julio sadly, rubbing gingerly at his bleeding head. The arrow's tip had taken a slim strip of flesh with it.

"You all right?" asked Dix.

"All right would be sleeping in the hay mound with no

Apaches for forty miles," Julio grumbled, bringing up his rifle again.

In the distance, Dix caught a blurry glimpse of two braves, running low from the second street down toward the first. Before he could utter a word, Julio had fired twice. The braves weren't running anymore.

While Dix's ears were still ringing, the old goatherd muttered, *"Dos perros.* You want to kill dogs, Cash, they are there for the killing."

"Golly," said Cash in admiration. "Nice shootin'!"

Grimly, Julio said, "There is more to do."

"Are you all right up there?" Nancy's worried voice echoed up the tunnel.

"So far," said Dix. Even though she was roughly thirty feet back, standing in the pitch black at the turn, he didn't need to shout.

Her voice strained, she said, "About Papagayo. It . . . it was my fault. I should have thought to make him a new leash after he lost his rope in the flood. I've made him a new one now. Melody and James are—" She gasped as another arrow shot through the tunnel and clattered against a side wall.

Cash fired immediately, twice, although Dix couldn't see what he was aiming at. He called back into the darkness, "You all right?"

"Yes!" Nancy wailed. "My God!"

Dix called, "Get back," then asked Cash, "Did you get him?"

Julio replied, "No target," before Cash had a chance to answer.

"Where's the bastard shootin' from, anyhow?" Dix asked. His eyes searched the little adobes, their edges, their windows and roofs, searched the weeds and the brambles.

Nothing.

He should have bought those damn glasses Doc Fedderson was always pushing at him. He should have brought his spyglass up here. And then he wondered if he'd put Yancy's saddlebags on Dasher, or his own. No, Yancy's. His spyglass should be back down the shaft with Nancy, in his packs.

Julio said, "He keeps us occupied while the others make a plan." He dropped his hand to touch the bulging outline of a box of cartridges, which he carried in his pocket. He had touched it several times in the last few minutes, Dix noted.

Scowling, Cash said, "I'd like to occupy him."

"Well, don't shoot unless you actually see somethin'," Dix said. "It's not like we're exactly swimmin' in ammunition. How much you got left for that old Smith & Wesson?"

Cash's eyes were on the town. "Maybe twenty rounds. Plenty."

"Not at the rate you're goin' through it."

"I only used up four rounds so far," Cash said defensively, then shrugged. "All right, five. But I got one of 'em." With the barrel of his gun, he pointed to one of the bodies that lay crumpled just outside the shaft. He smiled proudly.

"One Apache for five rounds," Dix said, nodding. He watched the distance, not Cash's face. Where was that sharpshooting archer, anyway?

"If you've got twenty rounds left," he went on, "and you stay true to what you did with the five slugs before, we can count on you to take out four more Apache. Four out of twenty or thirty. Hell, kid, you might's well go down the shaft and stay with Nancy and the youngsters."

Julio chuckled.

"All right, all right," Cash said angrily. "I get your point. I just— Shit!"

He ducked, shoving Dix down with him, as an arrow

whooshed overhead and clattered faintly on the wall at the end of the tunnel.

Julio fired, then scowled and swore softly in Spanish, *"¡Maldito!"*

"You see him?" Dix asked, peeking up over the table's edge again. Belatedly, he added, "Thanks, kid."

"Yeah," said Cash, as if it had been nothing.

"Only a movement in the brush, *señor,*" Julio said in disgust. "There, at the north edge of the graveyard. Maybe it was only the wind."

"Wind hasn't come up yet," said Dix. "Watch for him. You'll get him the next time."

"Sí."

Smoke began to rise from one of the caved-in frame houses, curling upward in a thick, gray black plume. Moments later, a second house went up, its wet timbers making for a good show.

His eyes still on the graveyard, Julio said, "They have started the burning." Slowly, he shook his head. "I hope my little goats have wandered far."

Suddenly, all the Mexicans were yammering full bore, but not a solitary one of them was talking to Yancy. The line of horsemen fell into Spanish, which he wasn't any great shakes at understanding, even when he heard it plain.

Likely, he thought dismally, they were arguing out the most entertaining method of killing Anglo deputies. At least there seemed to be some dissension within the ranks. One man was shaking his head, and another was drumming his fist against his thigh.

He wished he'd written his ma more often. He wished he'd kissed Marcy Evers, up in Gushing Rain. Cindy Hutchins, too. He wished a lot of things.

After a few moments, Alba turned back to him and asked in English, "How far?"

"What?"

"How far to this Regret?"

Yancy blinked. What the devil did Alba care how far it was? "Twenty-two, maybe twenty-four miles. To the south."

"There are only eight of us, Juan," said a man at the far end of the line, the man who had been shaking his head. "How many Apache?"

"My cousins will fight," volunteered a second man, ignoring the first. "They are not far, only at San Miguel. There are six of them. And they hate the Apache."

Yancy could scarcely believe his ears. He'd all of a sudden gone crazy, that's what it was! Too much sun and wind and rain had driven him around the bend.

"I am worth any two men," ventured another *bandido*. He pounded his chest with conviction and sat up straighter in his saddle.

"And I am worth three," said Alba, dead serious.

Yancy didn't think it was exactly the time to argue with him.

Alba said, "Pick up your boots, *gringo.*"

"You're gonna help?" Yancy asked. He didn't move. He was absolutely certain that the second he walked over there and bent to grab his boots, somebody'd shoot him in the back.

And laugh.

But Alba's face was hard. "Every man here has lost someone to the Apache." He pointed down the line to the man who'd said he had cousins at San Miguel. "Diego, his wife and son." He pointed to the next man. "Francisco, three nephews and his brother, Raul, who once rode at my side. Every man has only keepsakes when he would rather have the breathing flesh."

Alba spat down into the brush. "Apache dogs! I would

ride much farther than twenty-four miles to kill some Apache, *señor!*"

Still disbelieving, Yancy limped forward and gingerly reclaimed his boots. Nobody shot him.

He sat down, pulled the stickers out of his socks, and warily tugged his boots on. Nobody threw a rope around him and took off at a gallop.

All of a sudden, the world didn't make a damn bit of sense. Mexican bandits helping a white man? And a deputy at that! Maybe he had died during the night, and this was God's joke on him.

Or maybe he was still asleep. He'd wake up, and it would still be dark, and he'd be shivering and huddled underneath that blanket, running a fever of a hundred and ten.

But Alba pointed toward a man on a dun horse. "You ride behind Tomas. His horse is strongest. Tell me again how you get to this place."

He did, describing it the best he could, and then Diego took off for the southwest at a gallop, presumably to fetch his cousins. Toothless grabbed his horse's reins from one of the others and remounted, tossing Yancy's pistol back to him.

"Th-thank you," he stuttered as he shoved it into his holster.

All in all, Yancy figured that if this wasn't some sort of fever dream he was having, six or eight miles back to town, doubled, was a lot of miles to add to the twenty-some they'd have to ride to get back to Regret. And this bunch of tough, Apache-hating bandits—with the possibility of six more on their way—was a hell of a lot sounder proposition than the town boys he'd have to blackmail into coming.

It was a whole lot faster, too.

Tomas held his hand down, and Yancy clambered up on

the bony dun behind him, doing his best to ignore his wounds. His side was still seeping blood.

"We ride, *amigos!*" cried Alba. "We bring God's wrath down upon the murdering savages!"

With a great deal of yelping and whooping and a jolting start that finally convinced Yancy that he wasn't crazy or dreaming, they galloped into the south.

Julio fired.

This time, Dix saw the brave rise from the brush in shock and surprise. He fell face first, and ended sprawled between two tilting limestone markers, deader than a pork roast.

"Nice shot," Dix breathed admiringly. Julio was everything Nancy had claimed and more. If they got out of this mess, Dix was going to buy him a dozen jugs of whiskey and a brand-new hat.

He felt Cash bumping around and twisted toward him. The kid was panic-stricken and tugging feverishly at an arrow: an arrow that had gone clean through his shoulder and was poking out the other side.

"Calm down," Dix said curtly, and he snapped off the shaft. "Hold still."

He drew out what was left of the arrow by its head. The kid was scared to death, but he hadn't made a peep. He'd give him that.

He said, "Get back down the tunnel to Nancy and have her fix that up for you. Then we need you back up here again. And bring back my spyglass. It'll be in my saddle-bags."

Cash began to crouch his way back down the tunnel, and Dix said, "Wait. Take a lantern."

He handed one of their two to Cash. It was still burning.

It wasn't the only thing afire. All the wooden structures, both those that had already fallen and those that had been teetering on the edge of it, were aflame and smoking heavily, veiling the rest of the buildings. He could see little of the town.

For the first time in all his years in Arizona, he found himself wishing that the wind would come up.

Nancy looked up abruptly at the approaching footsteps, and was disheartened when they proved to belong to Cash instead of Dix.

Cash didn't appear to notice her disappointment, though. He put down his lantern, then pulled his other hand away from his shoulder. There was blood.

"Can you fix me up?" he asked, even as she worriedly gestured him down beside her.

"My medicine basket, James," she said. The children had been sitting quietly, the tethered and panting dog between them, ever since she'd brought Papagayo back.

Foolish dog. And she had been foolish, too, forgetting to tie him. If they died before help could reach them, it would be her fault.

"That's the one," she said when James put his hands on the third basket. He handed it over. She began to dig through it, saying, "Take off your shirt, please, Cash. Arrow, lance, or bullet?"

"Arrow, ma'am."

She found her sharp little knife, honed razor thin, and put a gentle hand on Cash's shoulder, studying the wound. And then she sat back. "Well, aren't you the fortunate lad!" she said in relief. She put the knife away. "It went all the way through, looks to be clean as a whistle!"

Melody put her little hand to her own shoulder in sympathy. "Ow," she said, making a face, and then crawled forward to pat Cash's hand. "Does it hurt bad?"

Both Cash's eyebrows shot up. "You're talkin'?" He looked over at Nancy. "She's talkin'?"

Nancy nodded curtly at Cash and said, "I'm sure it hurts quite a bit, Melody, but Cash is very brave." She handed the child a rag from her basket, and said, "Would you please wring this out in the water bucket?"

James, she noted, seemed to be eyeing Cash oddly. There was a trace of a smirking smile on his face, as if he were glad that Cash had been injured. It troubled her deeply.

"Melody started talking last night, didn't you, honey?" she said as the girl handed her the damp cloth. Gently, she began to wash Cash's wound—first the entry, then the exit.

Haltingly, Cash said, "I'd like to apologize again, ma'am. About . . . about the other morning. I wouldn't 'a shot you, honest."

Nancy smiled. "So you said. Several times. Consider it forgotten."

"I gotta say, though, you're a pretty fair hand with a knife."

She chuckled. "You've said that, too, but it's a good thing for you to remember. We Glasgow girls are wicked with a blade."

Cash's eyes got a little bigger. "You are?"

She held the laugh inside and clucked her tongue at him. "For heaven's sake, hold still!"

"Yes'm."

She took the tin of unguent out and lifted off the lid. "This may sting a bit," she said.

"Read a story?" Melody said.

Nancy dabbed the unguent on and around both wounds. "Your storybook washed away last night, I'm afraid," she said. Cash didn't flinch. "I'll tell you one in a little while, though. It's a story about a sleeping princess and a wicked witch and a handsome prince. Would that be all right?"

From the corner of her eye, she saw the girl smile, and gladness flooded her heart once again. For Nancy, joy followed the girl's every word. A miracle. James, on the other hand . . .

She put the tin of medicine away and pulled out a roll of bandages. "The worst part's over, Cash."

He relaxed.

"There's been no more shooting," she said, deciding the best way to wrap him. The arrow had gone through the narrow strip of flesh high on his shoulder, above the collarbone. It was a lucky wound, but it was difficult to know how to bandage it.

"No, ma'am," he replied. "I guess there ain't. Julio took out the son of a bitch what was shootin' at us. Sorry for the language, ma'am. They're busy torchin' the place right about now."

Her heart fell. She'd known they'd burn her house, the town, that they'd burn everything, but somehow the reality of it was a shock.

It must have shown on her face, because Cash put his hand on her arm. "Don't you worry, ma'am. Dix was real smart to barricade us in this mine, and I ain't never seen nobody that can shoot the way old Julio does. I reckon, what with the food you brung and the water, we can hold out for a good week if we have to."

"A week? But Yancy went for—"

"Don't listen to me, ma'am," Cash said quickly, cutting her off. "I was just rattlin'. Sayin' what ifs, you know?"

He was holding something back, but Nancy guessed that whatever it was, it wasn't coming out now. She began to bandage him, rolling the cloth down, under the opposite arm, then up, across his back.

"Last night," she said, "during the rain. When Dix brought Melody to me again, he had the oddest look on his face."

Cash raised his arm, to make the bandaging easier. "What you mean, odd?"

"I don't know, it was just strange. Rather whimsical. No, that's not right. A bit like he was someplace far away. Someplace very sad, but very happy. I can't explain it." She had only seen it for a second, but it had been there.

"Right after he pulled out Miss Pretty Face, there?" He smiled at Melody, and she gave him a shy grin.

"Yes." Nancy tied off the bandage.

"Reckon he was thinkin' about his own little gal," he said.

When Nancy stared at him, he added, "I don't know the whole story. My daddy said somethin' about it a long time ago. I guess Dix had him a Mex wife when he was sheriff-in' over to New Mexico."

He picked up his shirt. "There was somethin' about her goin' crazy and burnin' up herself and the kid," he said, matter-of-factly. "His wife set the house on fire or some-thin'."

His head disappeared for a moment while he pulled Enrique's blousy shirt over his head. It was just as well. He didn't see the look of shock and horror that Nancy couldn't keep from flickering over her face.

He shrugged into his sleeves, grimacing. "That's a right good job, ma'am. Thank you kindly."

16

Dix bit into his second piece of fried chicken, all the time keeping an eye to the outside.

Nancy had sent breakfast up with Cash. It seemed the ultimate incongruity that they should be hunched in an airless mine shaft, fighting off a deadly enemy that wanted nothing more than to skewer each and every one of them on a spit, while eating Nancy's biscuits and good chicken off of checkered napkins. But it tasted so good that he just kept eating.

If you were going to go, he figured you might as well go out well fed.

There had been no more sightings since Cash had taken the arrow, and that had been a while ago. They hadn't so much as spied another Indian.

This worried Dix. He would have thought they'd try to charge the mine. No, on second thought, they wouldn't. That would lose too many men. After all, the Apache had no idea of their numbers, and they'd already taken out at least five braves.

But by this time, the Indians sure as hell should have

tried to get in somehow. Of course, Dix didn't figure there was any way they could, but he also knew that you couldn't count on anything with Apache. Just when you thought everything was going your way, they turned it upside down and beat you to death with it.

He wondered about Yancy again, and couldn't keep his thoughts from turning grim. He wondered if his deputy was lying dead and mutilated on the plain, with the buzzards circling.

A shiver went through him, despite the nearly stultifying heat. Sweat poured from all three men, and the still air was so heavy with moisture that it didn't evaporate, not a bit of it. It ran down their backs in rivulets, soaked their clothing, made little damp spots that soaked into the wood where their hands touched the table barricade.

The heat was getting to him, that was all, he thought. Yancy was fine. Yancy was back in town. No, he'd already left and was heading toward them with a mob of men.

Or was he still trying to talk them into coming? Was he scouring the saloons and back alleys, looking for drunks who'd do anything—even agree to fight Apaches hand to hand—for whiskey money? Was he at the bank arguing with Old Man Peterson, giving him every good reason to send his men from the ranch?

Dix could hear Peterson now, sniffing haughtily behind that yellowed walrus mustache and those big white muttonchops. "It's none of my business, Deputy Ward, if Sheriff Granger wants to go clear out of his jurisdiction—miles out of it, I might add—and get himself tangled up with Apache. None of my business at all." And then he'd straighten his papers and huff dismissively.

The dumb bastard. He hoped Yancy pointed out that it was his bank robber they'd been chasing when they came across Regret. As if that would make any difference to Peterson.

"Crimeny," said the big bad bank robber, and Dix looked over at him. "I ain't never been so hot in all my borned days! I wish we could get this thing over with, just so's I could run down there and jump in what's left of the river."

"Not much in it but trees and dead fish by now, I think," Julio said philosophically. He had eaten exactly one chicken leg and two of those fried tortillas, downed nearly a half gallon of water, and resumed his watch.

"You take a look at that clock when you were down the shaft?" Dix asked.

Cash nodded, flicking three fat beads of sweat from his brow to Dix's shirt. "Quarter to ten. Probably after ten by now."

Dix figured it was about ten-fifteen. If it was this hot only halfway though the morning, it was going to be pure hell by afternoon. Nothing helped, not mopping the sweat on your soggy handkerchief, not moving around.

It was an old desert trick to hang wet towels in the doorways and windows and thus let the breeze cool the interiors of shacks and houses. But there was no breeze entering the shaft, at least, no more than a whisper. And even if there had been, it was so humid that nothing was evaporating.

He figured the only spot of cool in the whole town of Regret was down the well.

Outside, the wind had come up a touch. The smoke from the burning houses was fluttering slowly off to the southwest, across the town, across the river. They hadn't yet burned Nancy's house or the barn, so far as he could see, but that didn't mean anything. Adobe was nearly impossible to burn, but not the things in it. He'd seen smoke drifting lazily from the windows of Enrique and Soledad's house and heard the far-off pops of exploding glass. He figured it was the old loom and all that stuff in there with it.

But he still couldn't see any Apache.

To his left, there was a tiny breeze as Julio stood up and walked down the tunnel, into the shadows. He heard a sigh, and then a long spattering as Julio relieved himself against the wall of the shaft.

Cash sniffed the air and made a face. "Great. On top of everything else, I gotta smell his piss."

"You want to tell him to go outside and use the privy?"

Cash scowled. "Anybody ever tell you that you're real funny?"

With a grunt, Dix shifted his weight to his right knee. It felt like there was a team of angry dwarves hammering at his backbone. He said, "Yancy says I'm a laugh a minute."

"I'll just bet he does," said Cash.

The *bandidos* were afoot, walking their horses, and Yancy limped painfully behind them, struggling to keep pace. He comforted himself in the thought that he couldn't feel as lousy as Tomas's dun horse. It had been carrying two riders, was soaked and lathered, and walked with its head at about the level of its knees. Tomas didn't seem to care.

There was an argument up front. At least, he could hear the raised voices all the way back where he was, at the end of the line. He couldn't make out much, especially since it was in Spanish, but he picked out the word *"loco"* a couple of times.

Any way you looked at it, it wasn't the best omen.

Somebody signaled a stop—Alba, he supposed—and the horses in the rear, as well as the men on foot, slowly trailed up to meet the leaders. They all broke out water bags, and their horses drank thirstily.

Although Yancy had some disagreement with the manner in which the Mexicans treated their mounts, he had to admit that they had come farther than he had anticipated, and in much less time. They had long ago passed the spot where he'd turned Dasher loose. The horse was nowhere in sight, and Yancy hoped that he hadn't run into a hungry cougar. Old Dasher was in no more shape to take to his heels than he was.

Yancy figured that they were nearly a third of the way to Regret. Of course, they still had to climb through some rocky territory, and that was a slow business, but once they came into the canyon, they could go just about flat out. They couldn't get there soon enough to suit him.

He dug his watch from his pocket. A quarter to eleven. They might make it by five, four if they were lucky. He hoped their luck held.

With a grunt, Tomas shoved a canteen at him. Yancy nodded his thanks, then drank deeply, even though the water was hot and tasted faintly of alkali. It tasted, in fact, just like the water out at the seepage spot a few miles from Gushing Rain, where the Papago Indians came to plant crops once a year. He didn't like their water, either, not that he'd had to drink much of it. They made a real good beer, once you got used to it.

But a thirsty man didn't argue, nor did he ask questions. He drained the canteen.

Tomas took it back and frowned.

"There's tanks about three miles from here," Yancy said quickly, in his own defense. "Up in those hills." He pointed south, into the rocks toward which they were headed. "We can fill everything up again."

He didn't think it was the best time to add that the tank water was a tad buggy.

Whatever the bandits' argument had been about, it had escalated, because all of a goddamn sudden, somebody shot off a gun. Yancy jumped—as did Tomas and not a few of the horses—and he turned just in time to see Alba holstering his pistol.

Well, one of his pistols. He was double-rigged, with a gun on each hip, another stuck in his belt, and bandoliers crisscrossing his chest, and there was a great big Arkansas toothpick strapped to one thigh. He made Yancy feel positively underarmed.

Actually, they all did.

"¡Silencio!" barked Alba. He spoke more softly—but no less angrily—to the man who had been the most vocal during the argument. Yancy couldn't hear his words.

The man Alba had been addressing stiffened, then nodded curtly. Without a word, he swung up on his gelding, a bright chestnut, and stared down at the other men. In Spanish, he asked, "Who rides with me?"

Yancy understood that much, anyway.

He waited for a few tense seconds, and then suddenly, the man swore. "Fools!" he spat in English. Then he wheeled his horse toward the west and rode off at a lope.

"What was that about?" Yancy asked.

"He thinks there will be too many Apache," Tomas said, speaking for the first time, and dispelling Yancy's doubts about his command of the English language. "He is a coward. I never liked him, anyway." He turned the canteen Yancy had drained upside down and frowned. "There had better be tanks in those hills, Deputy."

Alba had remounted by this time, and slowly walked his horse the few steps to where Yancy stood, waiting. He studied the dun. He said, "Your horse will not last, Tomas."

Tomas nodded curtly. "I will ride him until he drops. I will have my pick of Apache horses."

Yancy opened his mouth, then closed it again.

But Alba had seen him. "You have something to say, Deputy? Maybe you think we should leave you behind, eh? Spare this horse?"

If Alba had expected some bleeding-heart plea about Tomas's dun, Yancy did not give it to him. He said, "I was just wonderin' when you were gonna give me back my badge."

Alba laughed. "I will think about it," he said. "Mount up, *compañeros,*" he announced to the group. "The trail is hot and long, but at the end we will spill much Apache blood."

One man hoisted his rifle and whooped, and then they all started shouting and hollering.

Not Yancy, though. He was trying, painfully, to clamber aboard Tomas's tired dun.

The dog's eyes were closed to pale blue slits that glowed eerily in the lamplight, his tongue lolled, and his pants echoed all around her. Nancy's throat was about to give out.

She had told the children six fairy tales, all of which they'd heard countless times before, although you wouldn't have known it by Melody's face. Then she'd launched into two long stories about the old country and recited a poem about a tiger, a poem she'd thought she'd forgotten long ago. About the only thing she had left was the saga of Bonny Prince Charlie, but she held back. Not only was she weary of talking, but the tale was too violent for children to hear, particularly children in these circumstances.

So she leaned back against the dirt wall, sweat clogging her every pore. Over the panting of the dog, she said, "Let's have a quiet time, shall we?"

She glanced at the clock before she closed her eyes. Twelve-thirty. The day was half gone, and so, in a manner of speaking, was she. Her hair was soaked and matted to her scalp and clotted with mud from the wall. The children were cranky and hot, and the stench of the slop bucket was a continual assault on her senses.

She wondered if the men had a breeze of any sort up there, in the front of the shaft. Back here, the lamp's smoke went straight up and pooled on the tunnel's ceiling like so much mercury. Not a breath of air.

"Nancy?"

She opened her eyes. "Yes, James?"

He stared at her flatly, perspiration trickling down his face, cutting pale lines through the dirt. His hair was plastered to his forehead, the blond of it darkened by sweat and earth from the tunnel's wall.

He said, "You have to hide Papagayo when the Apache come."

"They won't come back this far, James," she said soothingly, although James seemed little in need of comfort. She wished she knew what it was that he needed. "The men will stop them. We'll be just fine."

He studied her for a moment. "Hide him," he said.

By three o'clock, the breeze had come up at long last and it was headed their way. The smoke from the burning building, now rubble, had shifted direction. Now it was blowing toward them, although well overhead.

Cash closed his eyes for a moment. "That breeze helps some, I believe," he said. "Feel like I'm drownin' in here. Drownin' in boiling water."

Dix agreed wholeheartedly, although he said nothing. He just kept watching those buildings, or rather, the spaces between them. He wished just one of those damned redskins would show his face. A leg, an arm, anything to shoot at! Anything would be better than sitting here, waiting.

His nerves were beginning to show, he guessed. He felt as jumpy as a cat in a room full of rockers, and he was tired, so tired. He guessed he'd gotten maybe four hours' sleep, total, the last two nights. Sheriffing and fighting

Apaches weren't pastimes for old men, and he was feeling older by the second.

And when had that happened? he wondered. Sometimes it seemed he was Cash's age just yesterday, breaking broncs and rowdying it up with the fellas back home. Before he had pinned on a badge. Before he had met Ramona.

Sometimes it seemed a million years ago.

His head jerked up at a noise above. Julio had heard it, too. Both men eyed the tunnel's ceiling as the noises grew louder. Feet scuffling. Something heavy was moving or being dragged. Voices. There were Apache up there, all right, a whole lot of Apache, and this time they sure didn't give a damn who heard them. They'd come up behind the mine, probably walked north, out of sight, and circled around to the west.

What the hell were they doing up there?

"Hey, Sheriff?" Cash, who hadn't taken his eyes off the mouth of the tunnel, elbowed Dix in the side. "I take it back about that breeze."

A tumbleweed had been tossed down in front of the tunnel's opening, and ancient, splintered boards and more brush—half-dead brush, pulled up by the roots—and grass and weeds by the handful began to follow.

"Them bastards are gonna try an' smoke us out, ain't they?" Cash whispered in disbelief.

Nobody answered him.

17

When Yancy and the Mexicans were about a mile and a half away from entering the canyon, Diego showed up with not only a spare horse but six cousins and two extras. For the very first time, Yancy actually thought that he and Dix and the others might just live through this. All of the new men looked like they bit the heads off live badgers just for the sheer fun of it, and between them they carried enough weaponry and ammunition to outfit the Seventh Cavalry.

Alba seemed to know each of the new men, and he took advantage of the reunion to rest and water the horses. The Lord knew, they needed it. Yancy thought about suggesting to Tomas that he just leave his dun here, and that they ride the spare horse double. The dun was all in.

But Tomas was ahead of him. When Yancy glanced up—for he was lying flat on his back in the weeds, the only position in which his various aches and pains receded from a roar to a whisper—Tomas was stripping the tack from his dun. The horse, which hadn't been in exactly the best condition to start with, was worn down to a frazzle. Tomas had quirted its shoulders mercilessly for the last

couple of miles. Now it stood with its head low, its legs
and flanks quivering. Dark, shiny streaks of blood ran
from its neck and withers.

Yancy made a vow that if he came out of this in anything close to one piece, he was going to snag that dun
horse on the way home and feed him up good. He'd get
him nice and fat and sleek, all right. And then he'd sell him
to somebody who'd only ride him into town for church on
Sundays.

While he was thinking this over, the horse suddenly
groaned and fell to its knees, just fell right down.

Yancy sat up just as the horse went all the way over on
its side. Before Yancy could get his boots under him and
stand up, before he could get over there, Tomas casually
drew his pistol and put a bullet in the horse's brain.

As several of the horses made halfhearted attempts to
rear, Yancy yelped, "What'd you do that for?"

The dun had owned the boniest backside in four states,
but that wasn't his fault, and it sure wasn't any reason to
shoot him!

"All he did was lay down!" Yancy yelled. "I laid down
and you didn't shoot me!"

Tomas holstered his pistol. "I never like him, anyway,"
he said with a sneer. "You, I thought about shooting." He
turned and resumed saddling the new horse without a
backward glance.

Alba walked over. "How much farther?" he asked.

"Not much," Yancy said, angrily staring after Tomas.
"Six miles, maybe seven. That hatchet-faced, mossy-
toothed, horse-whippin', ungrateful son of a bitch!"

Alba shrugged. "He is all those things. But it was his
horse."

He started to rejoin the others, then paused, his eyes
flicking to Yancy's bandaged arm and his bleeding side.

Yancy supposed he was standing there pretty strange, too, on account of his hip, which hurt like a bastard.

Alba just kept staring, and Yancy snapped, "What?" and thought immediately that maybe it wasn't such a good idea to snap at a man like Juan Alba, especially when he was doing you a favor. And especially when he had as many side arms as Alba had strapped to his person.

But before Yancy could gulp, Alba said, "You are bleeding again, Little Deputy. Will you live to see *el campo de batalla?*"

The battlefield. Alba and his men were primed and ready, all right.

Yancy straightened as best he could and said, "I plan to give as much fight as she takes. More. And I ain't little."

Alba smiled slightly, his mustache twitching and his eyes dancing. "You are tall, anyway." He tipped his head toward the horses. "Come. Tomas waits. And I think the horse would have died anyway."

"I said to stop that, James," said Nancy, and she brushed at her sleeve again. Both her dress and her hand were dripping with perspiration, and her hand came away muddy.

"Didn't do anything," James repeated.

And then she felt it again. James hadn't been responsible. She was staring right at him. She wiped at the dirt again.

She looked up. "What in the name of—" A small clump of dirt hit her in the forehead.

On top of everything else, could this mine be haunted?

Stupid thought.

A small spat of dirt and gravel rained down from the ceiling again, clattering over her, pinging down over Soledad's mantel clock. The rains must have done it, she thought. The rains must have loosened some ancient fault in the soil and rock. Perhaps one of Julio's goats was up there, standing on it.

Maybe an Apache.

Softly, Papagayo began to growl.

"Get up, children," she said, keeping an eye on the ceiling. "Quickly, now."

"Hell's bells!" breathed Cash.

Tongues of flame had appeared at the sides of the brush pile that now all but covered the mouth of the mine. In very little time, the flames converged, and the sky disappeared. Dark smoke blotted it out, worked its way back into the mine shaft.

At first, there were just thin, wispy fingers of it, and Dix figured maybe that was all there would be, what with no draft to pull the smoke through. But then it came in slow billows as the fire took hold, feeding hungrily on the damp brush, and the wind began to push harder.

Coughing and rubbing at their tearing eyes, the men were forced backward, little by little.

Dix could hear the children behind him as the men backed toward the turn in the shaft, guns drawn, lanterns held high. He rounded the bend in the shaft. Melody was crying, James was muttering something about the dog, and Nancy was doing her best to comfort them. Her voice was close, too close.

He backed right into her.

"Dear Lord," Nancy said when she realized what the men were moving away from, and hurriedly turned the children around. "Quickly!" she urged.

The smoke followed them into the earth, down the shaft. Dix moved the group farther, past the place where Nancy had piled their supplies. They slowly angled downhill, going deeper and deeper. He suddenly realized they were walking through thick, sticky mud, and he could smell dank water, although he couldn't see it yet.

What would they do when they reached the water? Drown or choke to death. Neither choice offered much hope. Through the heavy air he could smell decay, growing thicker in his nostrils.

And then, with a start, he realized that the smoke wasn't as thick as it should be.

"Wait," he whispered, and touched Nancy's shoulder. She paused, a child under each hand. Cash and Julio stopped, too.

"The smoke," wheezed Julio.

"I know," said Dix.

"Where does it go?" the old goatherd asked before he coughed loudly.

Cash hissed, "Somebody want to tell me what's goin' on?" And then he doubled over, coughing.

"The ceiling!" Melody chirped almost happily through her dress. She held the hem of her skirt up over her mouth and nose, probably at Nancy's instigation. "It's going through our ceiling!"

"I don't think so, honey," Dix whispered. Maybe the Apache had kicked the fire apart and scattered the wood and brush.

Maybe they were already creeping down the tunnel.

He motioned Nancy and the kids to get in back of him, motioned Julio and Cash to the front.

"Dix," Nancy said urgently as she moved the children, "she's right! The ceiling—"

"Quiet!" he snapped, cutting her off. He had no time to waste on politeness. Something had made a noise up there, something that had scattered rocks and dirt with a clatter. He could still hear them falling.

Was that light he saw through his tearing eyes, or was it

a reflection of the lanterns, a trick of their muted glare on the smoke?

He held his lantern up. The smoke was drifting back up the tunnel, going the wrong way.

"I'll be jiggered!" he muttered under his breath, and then the faint light, which he had probably imagined in the first place, went out. The smoke was playing tricks on his eyes; that was it.

Next to him, Julio wordlessly set his rifle down, leaning it against the side of the tunnel, and drew his knife.

Everyone was coughing now, Dix included. It was no use telling them to stop or to be quiet. He just stood there, watching up the tunnel through watering eyes, waiting.

And then the dog growled. It was a low, warning sound, deadly serious, that abruptly changed to a deep bark as Papagayo ripped his makeshift leash from James's hands. Papagayo shot back up the tunnel and disappeared into the smoke as James cried, "No, no, no! Stop! Stop him, somebody!"

Immediately, there was the light again, high against the tunnel's roof and far forward, and at the same time it winked into view, someone screamed. Papagayo was frenzied now, gone crazy. Dix knew by the growls and frantic tearing that the dog had grabbed hold of an Apache and was giving him what for. Quickly, he motioned the others down to the floor.

Stealthily and with as much speed as he could muster, he moved back up the shaft. The light grew brighter with each step, and he left the lantern behind after a few feet.

The noise of the battling dog grew louder and louder. When Dix flicked a glance back, he saw Julio, who shrugged and said, "I followed. I never could take the orders."

And then Dix saw them. It was an Apache, all right, and Papagayo had hold of his knife arm. The man's blade had been knocked up the tunnel, out of reach, and blood flowed down his arm as well as his side and leg where Papagayo had raked—and was still raking—his teeth and nails into flesh, trying to gain purchase.

The Apache wasn't beating at Papagayo with his fist, as Dix would have thought. He actually looked scared of the dog—terrified, more like—and seemed to be frantically trying to get free of him, to push him away and escape. The two whirled round and round in what Dix could now tell was light from above. The damn shaft had caved in and made them a chimney!

Smoke vented up the hole as Dix tried to get a clear shot. He didn't want to hit the dog, but Papagayo and the brave were dancing so fast on the pile of rubble that had fallen through that he couldn't get a shot off.

And then he heard James, just as the boy ran past him, heard him shout, "No, no, Papagayo! Bad dog! Bad dog!"

Dix reached to grab him, but only brushed a fleeting bit of his shirt. Julio grabbed for him, too, but had no more luck.

Dix had no choice. He lurched forward. He only had about fifteen feet to go, and he caught James's collar right off and pitched the boy backward with all his might. He heard an "oof!" right off—he'd likely tossed him smack into Julio—but he didn't have time to look. He'd already caught the brave's left arm and swung him around.

Sweat and grease made the Indian nearly impossible to hold onto, and he was screaming something in Apache and slamming the dog's body into Dix's ribs to boot. But Dix managed to get the barrel of his Colt jammed into the Indian's chest just long enough to pull the trigger.

As the Apache brave crumpled, the dog let go of his savaged forearm and backed off, panting for a second, then cocking his ears and looking upward, toward the little hole in the ceiling.

That soft, low growl again.

Suddenly, there was no light.

Disoriented, Dix tripped in the darkness, stumbled over the dead Indian and the growling dog, and fell headlong into the wall of the tunnel, narrowly missing a wooden support. He went down on his knees. And at the instant there was light again, he felt all the air leave his lungs. Somebody had jumped him, whooping a terrible war cry next to his ear.

Dix rolled hard to the side and shot out an arm, just catching the Indian's wrist before the blade could do more that scratch his chest. A shot echoed in his ears, more dirt fell, and the brave went limp. Papagayo gave a last growl and let go of the brave's shoulder, leaving deep tooth-marks.

There was a small shower of rocks, and Dix shoved the inert body off himself in time to see the last of the smoke curling from the barrel of Cash's Smith & Wesson. Nancy was beside him, Melody clinging to the back of her skirts. Julio was just getting to his feet behind her, his hand on the dog, who was covered in blood.

Julio grunted, "I think you had better not sit there, *amigo.*" Dix moved just as a spear flew down the hole and, with a quick, sick sound, buried itself in the body of one of the dead braves.

"Jesus!" Dix tried to mutter between clenched teeth, but he had no air with which to say it.

He heard Nancy cry, "James! James, what on earth!" and looked away from the dead Indians to see her kneeling down toward the boy.

"You didn't hide him, you didn't hide him!" the boy repeated angrily, his eyes wet with tears. The dog tried to lick his face, but James pushed him away.

Dix finally got his air back with a whoosh that hurt his chest, but he was grateful just to be breathing. He signaled to Julio and Cash to keep watch on that beam of light, just in case anybody else was stupid enough to slide down the hole, and then he got to his feet and walked back to Nancy.

"Where could I hide him, laddie?" Nancy was soothing. "He wouldn't have fit in my pocket, now would he?"

"You didn't hide him," the boy wailed. "Didn't you see that first one's face? How scared he was? Now they'll never take us!"

18

Yancy and the bandits were loping through the canyon, pacing themselves, when Yancy saw the smoke. To the south, where the sky met the canyon's rim, it hugged the distant rocks like a living black cloak, fluttering softly to the southeast.

Sickly, his heart rose up into his throat at his first glimpse of it. They were burning. Didn't they usually wait until they'd killed every last living thing to burn the place? He didn't know.

He didn't have much experience with Apache, just things he'd heard from this one or that one. He didn't know how much of what he'd heard were lies or braggadocio, but even if a tenth of it were true, it was enough to send the hairs on the back of his neck to prickling.

He was about to yell in Tomas's ear, about to point toward the smoke, when somebody up front yelped and the whole crew picked up speed. It could have been any man of them, and they were so enveloped in dust that he couldn't see anything, anyway. Yancy and Tomas were at the back, and Tomas's new horse labored beneath them.

The pack was swiftly leaving them behind. He could see that, anyway.

The wind tearing at his face, Yancy put his mouth next to Tomas's ear and yelled, "It's not—"

Tomas's arm shot out and gave Yancy a tremendous shove to the side.

Startled, Yancy fell. He felt a whoosh of air as the horse's pistoning hooves barely missed his face. He managed to flap his arms twice, for what little good it did, and then he landed flat on his back. A tremendous groan of pain and surprise and anger burst from his lungs at the impact.

He lifted his head just in time to see Tomas spurring the horse onward. In less than a second, Tomas had disappeared into the roil with the others. He didn't even have the decency to give a backward glance.

Yancy let his head drop back with a thump. Damn that Tomas, anyway! He'd just been going to say that it wasn't far, that was all!

He lay there a minute or so, panting and taking stock of his injuries, and he finally decided that he hadn't busted anything new. With a pained growl, he managed to get to his feet.

He wavered for a moment, then started slowly limping toward the end of the canyon, limping toward Regret with the wind beating at his side, and cursing under his breath with every faltering step he took.

"Well, that ain't gonna work," said Cash. He slumped against the wall, back down into the solid slick of mud that carpeted the tunnel.

Dix scowled at him, blinking when another thick rivulet of sweat ran into his eyes. Every time one of them tried to sneak forward and snag a water bottle, a spear or a hail of arrows or a rifle blast came down the hole.

This last time, Dix had tried to hook the barrel of his outstretched rifle through the water bucket's handle and pull it toward him. He figured wash water full of clotted mud was better than no water at all. But when another arrow came down to skewer his borrowed and already mistreated hat to the floor, he'd backed up in disgust.

"We'll wait a while and try again," Dix said, eyeing his hat. He sat back and mopped his brow, for what little good it did him. His bandanna came away black.

Beside him, Julio crouched on his heels, his rifle across his knees. "These Apache, they are true hat killers, no?" he said with just a trace of a grin, and thumbed his arrow-ripped sombrero.

"Oh, you're real funny," Cash muttered disdainfully. "Hardy-har-har."

"Everybody, calm down," Dix said, although he said it mainly for Cash's benefit. "We'll get our water. We'll get our food. And that hole is lettin' out smoke like the good Lord meant it for just that purpose."

He didn't add that the smoke from the front of the shaft had thinned out quite a bit, and that the Apache had most likely kicked apart that bonfire they'd built. Those braves were sure taking their sweet time, though. They knew they had this little band of whites and Mexicans trapped, just as they'd trap a badger in its den and poke it with sticks till it got mad enough—and foolish enough—to charge out.

He also didn't mention that their ammunition was somewhere beneath that dusty, smoky beam of light, as well. Just fifteen feet away, it was buried under the hump of the cave-in's rubble.

The Apache had trapped them as surely as any windstorm, as surely as the torrent the night before. They were another force of nature, with the distinction that they had deadly intent. The wind just blew and the rain and hail just fell, and if a man happened to be in the way, he got pounded the same as any cactus or rock. But the Indians above, the Indians outside, had one purpose: to obliterate them.

It wouldn't be too awfully long—maybe a couple of hours, maybe a few minutes—before they'd be knee deep in Apache.

Leaving Julio and Cash to keep a lookout up the mine, he skidded back down the shaft, into the shadows, to check on Nancy and the children. Papagayo, his coat still smeared with Apache blood, greeted him with a happy thump of his half tail. His blue eyes glowed in the lantern light. Dix put down his hand to scratch the dog under his chin and behind his feathery ears.

"Good fella," he said softly. "You give 'em what for, all right, Papagayo?"

"Papagayo's our hero," said Nancy. Melody was under her arm, and looked up wistfully. Lord, she had a sweet little face. With his thumb, he wiped a little of the grime from her forehead. Or he tried to. His hand left a muddy smear.

She smiled up at him, anyway. "Where's your hat?" she asked.

"Don't tell me I lost it again!" he said, feigning surprise, and felt his head.

Melody laughed. Music.

"Best dog hero I've seen for a spell," said Dix, tearing his gaze from Melody and centering it on Nancy. She was as muddy and soaked with perspiration as any of them, but she smiled. Strangely, it lightened his heart a good bit. "The craziest-lookin' hound in four counties," he said, "but the best. How's James?"

The boy, seated a few feet away from Nancy, didn't so much as glance up.

Nancy just shook her head. Her smile was gone.

Gently, Dix said, "Like to have a word with you, son." He planned to give the boy a mission, something to occupy his mind. He planned to tell him that when and if the Apaches charged them, James was in charge of getting his sister and Nancy farther down the shaft and into the water. But James didn't give him a chance.

The boy looked up long enough to hiss, "I'm not your son." His eyes filled with cold hatred. "I am Tábano's son."

Although Nancy shifted with a jerk, Dix didn't blink. If James wanted to have this out here and now, he was willing. He said, "This Tábano. He's the fella that dropped you off here, right?"

The boy was breathing rapidly, angrily. "His woman died. He said it would be better for us. He was old. But he said that someday he'd see us again."

Dix figured that Tábano had likely meant they'd be reunited in the happy hunting grounds, but he said, "Tábano? What's that mean?"

"A fly," the boy answered curtly. "It means a horsefly. That's the Mexican. The Apache name's a secret from the likes of you."

Nancy started to scold the boy, likely for talking back, but Dix held up his hand and silenced her before she got two words out. He kept looking at the boy and nodded sagely. "I see. So, you reckon Tábano's sent these boys to pick you up?"

"Yes," said James defiantly. Then, "No. I don't know. Doesn't matter anymore." He dropped his eyes.

Nancy said, "James? Why not?"

James didn't answer.

"James," Dix said, "I'm gonna talk straight to you. Think you're man enough to handle it?"

The boy raised his head again, meeting Dix's gaze with a stony stare that made him look more twenty-two than eleven. No child should ever look like that, Dix thought, and sorrow flooded his heart. No child should ever have the experience to even *think* to look like that.

"These Apaches didn't come for you, James," Dix said evenly. "They don't even know you're here. They came because Soledad killed one of their pals. Right or wrong, she did it, and now we're having to pay the price. Your friend, Tábano, might have taken good care of you for a while, but you were only in his care because the Apaches killed your mama and daddy."

"No," said James.

Melody whimpered.

"If you'd been a little older," Dix said, "they would have killed you, too."

"No!"

"Likely, Tábano dropping you off is the only thing that's kept you alive. He knew he couldn't protect you any-more. You kids are gettin' old enough that pretty soon they'd use you for target practice, James, and marry your little sister off to the man with the most ponies."

James leapt to his feet. "Stop it!" he shouted angrily, both to Dix, and to Melody, who was wailing by this time. "You're lying! Liar, liar!" And then he burst into a brittle torrent of Apache.

Dix had no way of knowing if all that stuff he'd said was true, but he waited until the boy ran down and Nancy quieted the girl, and then he said, "See? That's just what they're afraid you'd do, James. One of the things, anyhow. Don't you know that the Apache think it dirties their tongue for a white man or a Mexican to hear it spoken? Isn't that why you couldn't tell me Tábano's true name?"

This, at least, Dix knew to be a fact.

James's eyes grew wide in horror at the sin he'd just

committed. The hate was still in there, but now it was confused. And at least the boy was silent.

"That dog's another thing, isn't it, James?" Dix asked, his voice steady. "How come that Apache looked so scared of him?"

"Dix, stop it," Nancy warned. She held Melody close.

He ignored her. "Any other man would have ripped Papagayo's head clean off, but that brave appeared to just want to get away from him."

"His eyes," the boy said defiantly. Suddenly, he bent and picked up a rock from the floor, and threw it at Papagayo with all his might. "I hate you, I hate you, you blue-eyed ghost!"

The dog yelped and fled up the shaft, toward Julio and Cash.

Dix heard the distant sing of an arrow, and Papagayo howled pitifully.

Dix scrambled forward, slipping on the mud, leaving Nancy and the children behind. In the seconds it took him to join Julio and Cash, the dog had crawled nearly out of the spot of light. The arrow had sunk deep into his hip.

Cash had left his position at the wall and leaned forward on his knees, coaxing, "C'mon, boy! C'mon, old fella."

A second arrow took Papagayo in the shoulder, and he yelped with a scream that echoed up and down the damp tunnel walls. Dix heard laughter from above, beyond the light, and he swore.

"Come, *muchacho!*" cried Julio urgently over the echoes, over the dog's frantic whines. "I will give you tortillas and chicken, all your favorites!" Softly, pleadingly, he whispered, "Come, you bag of bones."

Before Dix could stop him, Cash threw himself forward, sticking his head too far into the light, firing

blindly upward with his right hand and grabbing the
dog's front legs in his left. As the shots reverberated, he
yanked back, pulling the screaming dog with him. Two
more arrows and a rifle slug sang down, embedding
themselves with three sharp *spats* in the dirt that Papagayo had just vacated.

Julio cradled the dog's body, and Cash hissed, "Goddamn heathens! Shootin' a poor dog and laughin'! And
somebody better kill that crazy son of a bitchin' kid. We
heard him yellin' at this dog clear up here! Is Papagayo
hurt bad, Julio?"

"I cannot tell," Julio replied, worriedly stroking the
dog's head. He whispered, "Rest easy, *mi corazón*," before
he looked up again. "He is alive, anyway."

Dix held out his arms. "I'll take him to Nancy," he said
curtly. "And shut up, Cash. Last night you were punchin'
him in the head."

"That was different," Cash grumbled.

Dix took the dog from Julio. "Get back to watchin' the
shaft." The last thing he needed was everybody so shook
up about the damned dog that they didn't keep their eyes
peeled for trouble.

He didn't mention that Cash had just spent another four
rounds getting Papagayo back, four rounds they couldn't
afford to spare.

Nancy was already on her feet when he got back. She
took Papagayo from him and laid him gently on the muddy
floor, muttering, "Poor laddie, poor laddie." Melody bent
to him, too.

James was still standing where Dix had left him, hands
balled into shaking fists at his sides. But he was crying
soundlessly as he watched Nancy labor over the whimper-
ing dog. She broke off one of the arrow shafts, and Papagayo yelped and snapped his teeth at the air, then went
back to pitifully licking Melody's hand.

Dix looked at James for a long time before he said, "You hate him and you love him. That's a hard thing for a feller to stand up to, isn't it?"

Slowly, without looking at him, James nodded. "I didn't want to love him." Tears streamed down his face then, cutting fresh pale paths through the grime. "He has blue eyes, see? He's a ghost dog. A spirit dog." One fist came up to grind at his eyes. "Is he gonna be all right?"

Suddenly, Dix understood. James had wanted to go back to the Apache with all his heart. He'd probably been with old Tábano and his wife for longer than he'd been with his real folks. He wanted to go back in the worst way. Except that Indians tended to get real spooked by ghosts, and if they thought any blue-eyed dog was a spirit . . .

For an eleven-year-old boy, it would have been a soul-wrenching decision. James probably figured that he could live with strangers and have the dog he loved, the one true thing in all of his short life, or go with the people he held as friends and return to the only way of life he'd known. But to do that, he'd have to forever leave behind the love and steadfast adoration that the dog gave him freely. The same dog that now lay next to them, bleeding into the mud.

Dix supposed that old Papagayo was the only thing that James had ever let get close enough to love him. As it was, the boy was shaking so hard that Dix was afraid he'd fall down.

"Papagayo?" the boy said, and his voice was very thin and high, not like James at all. "Nancy? I'm sorry, Papagayo."

A glance over at Nancy told Dix she'd heard every word and understood much more. Her eyes met Dix's, and they were full of unspoken things as she said, "Come help us, James."

Dix was about to kneel to the dog, too, when the echoing blast of another shot shook the tunnel walls.

"Gotcha, you red bastard!" cried Cash.

His side arm drawn, his boots sliding on the mud, Dix ran forward.

19

Dix didn't need to ask Cash what was going on.

By the time he had Cash and Julio in sight, he could see the Apaches swarming toward them. He fired as he ran, his third shot cutting down a man being lowered, upside down, through the hole in the tunnel's ceiling. The Apache swung there for a moment, lifeless, the blood dripping down his arm and off his fingers, before his comrades pulled him up again.

That was just the side show, though. Most of the Indians were coming from up the tunnel. Cash and Julio had accounted for two more bodies in that pool of light on the floor, but arrows continually sang toward them from across it. They were plastered against opposite walls, weapons outstretched, firing when they dared a shot.

"C'mon, you heathen cowards!" Cash called almost hysterically. "Show your ugly faces!"

In reply, an arrow whooshed through the beam of light, driving deep into a wooden support inches from Cash's face. Shaking, he eyed it.

Dix, who had pushed up against the wall at Julio's back,

shouted, "Get hold of yourself, boy!" and motioned up toward the hole with the barrel of his Colt.

This time, all three men fired as one, and a new assassin, whose head had just popped into sight, was stilled. The men above must have lost their tenuous grip on his greased legs, because they dropped him. The dead brave slowly slithered, then fell the rest of the way to the floor. With a soft thump, he landed atop his brethren, crumpled like a rag doll.

Immediately, Dix heard a whistle—a little bird call, but man-made—from above. There was a scuffling sound from the tunnel beyond the light, and then it was quiet again.

"You think they go, *señor*?" Julio whispered after a moment. Dix figured that the old man couldn't get any closer to that wall if he were pasted to it.

"What do you think?" Dix asked, wiping sweat from his face. It was likely only ninety degrees down here, but it felt like a hundred and twenty and everything stank: the slop bucket, the mud, himself, and the others, and he could smell Nancy's fried chicken going bad.

Dix had backed off some and was crouched on the muddy floor, panting in that steaming, stinking air. He was dog tired, and every single part of him hurt.

He reminded himself that he could hurt a whole lot worse, though, if he dropped his guard for more than a second.

Julio, too, inched back to hunch beside him. "For me, I think they are only gone for a little while," he said. "I fear they have plans." He shook his head, and large drops of perspiration flicked every which way. "I do not like Apache plans."

Dix looked up the tunnel at Cash. Still trembling, he was rooted to the spot, that old Smith & Wesson of his cocked and at the ready.

"Cash," Dix said softly.

There was no reply, and he was about to say the boy's name again when, in a strangely high voice, Cash said, "There's so many of 'em! How can there be so many? Six dead, right here on the floor, and five more dead outside!" He turned his head back toward Dix and said, "Why don't they just give up? Are they crazy? Has everybody gone crazy?"

The light from above flickered, and Dix yelled, "Get down!"

Cash didn't. Before he had time to slither to the mud-slick floor, Julio had cut down yet another brave coming through the vent in the ceiling. But it wasn't in time. When Cash hit the ground, there was an arrow in his side.

"I'm dead, I'm dead!" Cash howled.

Dix said, "Cover me," and while Julio fired alternately at the ceiling and the shaft beyond the light, Dix scrambled across the tunnel and dragged Cash backward, past Julio, around a slight bend in the tunnel. He didn't stop until they were in the safety of the shadows.

"Am I dead?" Cash asked, when Dix had pulled him to cover. "It hurts!"

Dix was busy running his fingers down the arrow's shaft. "Shut up," he snapped. "You're makin' too much noise to be dead."

"Dix," he heard Nancy say just before he felt her hand on his arm. She had left the children and the dog to meet him halfway. She was smart to have spoken before she touched him. In the state he was in, he likely would have lashed out first and asked questions later.

"He's all right," Dix said. He wrapped his hand around the shaft and gave it a little tug. Cash let out a yelp, but the arrowhead came free easily.

"I'm dyin'!" he shouted again, and Dix grabbed him by the collar.

"You don't shut up, you will be dyin', 'cause I'm gonna kill you!" he snarled, then remembered himself. "Arrow didn't sink in much. You got ribs as hard as your head."

Blinking, Cash felt his side. "I do?"

Dix dragged him to his feet, then bent and picked up the bloody arrow he'd just pulled out. He snapped it over his knee, breaking it into two pieces, one long, one short, and tucked the short end with the attached arrowhead into Cash's pocket. "Show that to your grandkids," he said more kindly. "Now get back up with Julio."

Cash, who had been staring at his pocket, looked up, wide-eyed. "Ain't she gonna fix me up?"

"I can't do more than Dix has," Nancy said quietly.

Dix nodded. "They still got men up top, and—"

"No foolin'," Cash breathed snidely, his hand to his side.

"And probably left another one watchin' on the other side of the light, up-tunnel," Dix went on. "So don't get cocky." He turned toward Nancy. Here the old tunnel was deep in gloom, halfway between the cave-in's light and lantern's glow, far back. But he could make her out. Somehow, she still managed to look pretty, even with her dress covered in mud, and soot and sweat streaking her face and matting her hair.

He wished he'd met her anyplace but here. Someplace nice, where nobody was shooting at him, where nobody even thought to. Someplace cool. Of course, she probably wouldn't have given him a second glance. Beautiful women rarely did.

He said, "How's everything back there?" He meant the children, he meant Papagayo, and most of all he meant not to ask that question at all, but to tell her that he was fond of her, that he admired her courage and kindness and the way she put things when she talked to him, and that he wanted to get to know her better, if these damned Indians

would only go away. That he wished things had been different.

But as usual, the words were lost to him.

"I won't ask you what's been happening," she said softly,
there in the half light. "You're all alive, and that's what mat-
ters. If we make it through, you can tell me all about it later.
Over a long dinner. If not . . . ?" She shrugged. He couldn't
read her expression. "I'll die knowing that you tried with all
your might to save us, all three of you. I'll go to my Maker
with the knowledge that I have been privileged to know far
more than my share of good men, brave men."

Again, she left Dix speechless. What could he say to
that?

Apparently she didn't mean that he should say anything, because she went on, "James is better, I think. What
you said to him . . . It was hard, but no harder than our circumstances. He needed to hear it, I suppose. I just didn't
have the heart."

And then she straightened. "Papagayo wasn't so seriously injured as I first thought. I'll need my special knife
to dig the arrowheads out, though. I don't suppose
you've—"

"Not yet," Dix said. Why couldn't he say a simple sentence to this woman? Why couldn't he say, "Nancy, I admire you," or "Nancy, I've grown awful fond of you"?

Hell, they'd probably all be dead inside an hour, and
then it would be too late, wouldn't it? Yancy wasn't coming with the citizenry of Gushing Rain; it was past the time
for that. The cavalry wasn't going to come charging down.
No one was going to rescue them.

He knew what he'd do if he were one of those Apaches.
They had probably already thought of it, too.

So he just said, "I'll see what I can do."

"Thank you," she said, and then she just stood there,
like she was expecting him to say something else.

"Oh, honestly," she muttered, and then, before he knew what was happening, she stepped forward and kissed him, just a lingering brush of soft lips, tinged with sweat and grief, but good, so good. Before he could put his arms around her, she stepped away. "I'll pray for you, laddie," she said.

"Th-thanks," he replied dumbly, blinking in surprise, just as another shot rang out up the tunnel. He turned and ran toward it. He almost welcomed it.

He slid against the wall, behind Cash, in time to see one of the braves' bodies slowly slither off the pile and into the darkness on the other side. Julio, who apparently had fired the first shot, sent another bullet into the dark.

"*Mierda,*" Julio cursed softly, and opened the old Winchester's magazine. He thumbed the box of cartridges from his pocket and began feeding them into his rifle's chamber. "They are taking their dead. This is either a very bad thing or a good one. *Muy malo,* I think."

Dix nodded. He had enough Spanish to understand that, anyway. *Very bad.*

Like Julio, Dix couldn't see these boys just giving up and going home. They'd lost too many men to do that. The Apaches, who prided themselves on skill and stealth and cunning—and on losing few warriors in battle—had been shamed. And they were going to be even more ashamed when they pulled the white and Mexican carcasses out of this tunnel and found a grand total of six, counting a woman and two kids.

He hoped it embarrassed the living shit out of them.

"What you think they're gonna do next?" Cash whispered. His side was still bleeding, but he'd calmed down a good bit.

"Finish pullin' those bodies out," Dix said, just as someone tossed a rawhide loop into the light. It snagged one foot of the topmost body.

Cash and Julio both fired, but the loop tightened, and slowly, the body was dragged out of sight, down off the mound of rubble and bodies and out of the light.

"How many rounds you fellas got left?" Dix asked. Somebody was going to have to go out into that bright beam of dusty light and get more ammunition. He supposed that somebody was him. He just hoped Julio and Cash had enough bullets left between them to cover him.

Cash felt his belt loops, then gave a nervous laugh. "Just what's in the gun. Guess you were right, Sheriff."

Julio tossed his empty cartridge box to the floor, and said, "Fourteen. My magazine is almost full."

"All right," said Dix, crawling slowly forward. "I've got a surprise for you, Cash. We've got plenty of bullets for that old gun of yours, if I can just get to 'em."

Angrily, Cash began, "But you told me—"

"Shut up," said Dix. "I'm gonna make a dive for the ammo, and I want you boys to cover me. And when I get back, Cash, I want you to tell me why you robbed that bank."

"What?" Cash said. "It's just one thing after another with you, isn't it?"

"Humor me," Dix said. He wasn't looking at Cash, but at that big mound of dirt and rocks and Apache mothers' sons, and trying to remember where Nancy had moved the box when the tunnel flooded. He said, "If I'm gonna meet my Maker over fifty lousy dollars and change, I'd kinda like to know why. Julio, you fire low, across the light. I trust you not to shoot me in the ass. And Cash, you put some slugs up through that hole."

"Aw, Jeez," grumbled Cash.

"Ready," said Julio, and he pressed the rifle's stock to his shoulder.

Dix leapt forward, and at the instant he did, all hell broke loose. Gunfire shook the walls of the tunnel, deafening him and showering him with rocks and debris shaken loose by the vibrations. He crawled to the place where the earlier cave-in had all but buried their supplies, and he began to dig feverishly.

Just as he uncovered the top of the ammunition box, he saw a movement to his side and realized that somebody had thrown the rawhide loop again. The unseen Apache, down on the other side of the mounded rubble and fearless in the face of gunfire, had missed. He was quickly reeling it back for another try.

With a yelp of "Heads up!" Dix threw himself to the side, grabbed it, and hauled back, hard, pitching himself from the edge to the center of the beam of light. He felt a slug whiz past his ear, and yelled, "Damn it, Cash!" just as the Apache at the other end of the line surfaced, then let go.

He fell backward at the sudden slack in the line, drew his Colt, and fired before he hit the ground. He saw the Apache grip his shoulder and stagger backward, then drop out of the light as someone else shot him in the chest, dead center.

Dix tossed his pistol over his head, back toward Cash and Julio, thinking he could throw it faster than holster it, and then he threw himself over to the side and grabbed the ammunition box with both hands.

He scrambled backward, pausing only to snag his poor hat, and he didn't stop scrambling until he was well back from the light. He yelled, "We're all right, Nancy," down the tunnel before he remembered that he hadn't got her little medical basket.

In a wavering voice, she called an echoing, "Thank God!"

The others crept back after him. Cash, who had been using Dix's gun, handed it back, empty. Julio took another box of ammunition, and Cash dumped the spent cartridges from his handgun and started loading again.

"Well?" said Dix, still out of breath. He turned his hat over in his hands and pulled the arrow from it. For being pinned to the ground and having two Apaches fall on it, it didn't look as stove up as a man might expect. He gave the shredded brim a roll, then settled it on his head.

"*¿Qué?*" asked Julio. He paused to wipe his sleeve across his face. "*¡Dios mío!* In all my years, I have never been so hot. And I have been very hot, *señores.*"

Dix grabbed the box Cash had just finished with and started seeing to his weapon. "She's a bitch, all right. Seems to me that Cash, here, was gonna tell us why he robbed the bank in Gushing Rain, weren't you, Cash?"

Cash said, "Hadn't we best get back up there?"

Dix swung his Colt's cylinder closed with a click. "Tell."

Cash glanced nervously up the tunnel. "I got a gal, all right?"

Dix said, "And?"

"She's over to Yuma."

"And?"

"Name's Cindy Mofford."

"If you do not hurry, *mi amigo,*" Julio broke in, "I think we will all be dead." To Dix, he said, "You will excuse me. I do not care why he robbed the bank." He scuttled up the tunnel, a box of cartridges in one hand and his rifle in the other.

Cash remained silent.

"How the hell did you get a gal over in Yuma?" Dix insisted. "You haven't been out of town but twice in your life!"

Unlike Julio, Dix didn't believe they were in any immediate danger of being swamped by Indians. They'd have to regroup and replace the brave that he'd shot, and then they'd still have to haul out those bodies, one at a time. At least, they'd have to if they were up to what he thought they were up to. He was grateful for the respite. "Well?" he said.

"I just met her, that's all," Cash said grudgingly.

"And she told you to rob the bank."

"No!" Cash's eyebrows shot up in horror. "She's a real lady! But she's . . . she's kinda used to nice things." He looked to the side. "I ain't got much, you know? Anyhow, she wrote and said as how her pa couldn't help but let her marry a man who could buy her a fine four-year-old pinto ridin' horse for forty-five dollars."

Dix raised a brow, and a fat drop of sweat fell into his eye. He blinked it away, but it just kept dripping. Maybe the hat hadn't been such a good idea, after all. "A four-year-old pinto for forty-five bucks? Kinda specific, wasn't she?"

"Oh, she had him all picked out."

Dix waved a hand in front of his face in an attempt to create a breeze. It didn't help. "I'll just bet she did."

Cash scowled. "What you mean by that?"

"I mean that you wrecked your whole dad-blamed life so that a spoilt girl could have a pony, that's what I mean! Just what did you two intend to live on once you spent all the money on her goddamn horse?"

Cash took a long breath, then winced. His hand went to his side. "Didn't think about that, I guess."

Dix got to his feet and held his hand down to Cash. There were still faint red cuff marks on the boy's wrists from yesterday. There was blood from the arrow he'd taken this morning—and more from the other he'd taken this afternoon—on his too-small, borrowed white shirt. Now it was sweat-gray in places, mud-brown in others, and thoroughly soaked in perspiration.

Cash was having a bad day, all right, and it was going to get worse in more ways than one. It was a day for hard truths.

"Well," Dix said, "you might want to consider that once she got that little pinto, she'd've probably jilted you faster than you can say 'spit.'"

"No, she wouldn't! I was hopin' that—"

Dix cut him off. "And she's the same as got you killed. I'd say that's one selfish little gal you got there, Cash."

Cash gained his feet, but he grabbed hold of Dix's arm. "Get me killed? But . . ." Suddenly, he sobered. "You don't think your deputy's comin' back, either, do you?"

Dix shook his head. Quietly, he said, "He rode north. Those first braves, yesterday morning. They came down from the north."

"That doesn't mean—"

Dix cut him off. "If he was comin', he'd be here by now. My watch got wrecked, but I can tell it's gettin' late by the angle of that light comin' down from up top. Yancy should have got to town by four or so yesterday afternoon, which would have given him all night to round up a posse and be ready to ride out at dawn. If he was comin', he should've been here by four. Five at the latest. I reckon it's about six by now."

"But more men—town men—would take longer to get *anywhere!*" Cash said in desperation, and then he slumped. Eyes to the ground, he added, "I reckon I knew it all along. I reckon there ain't but five fellers in town who'd come without a gun to their heads." He looked up. "That's true, too, ain't it, Sheriff?"

Dix didn't say anything.

"Then why'd you send him in the first place?"

Dix sighed long and hard. "I guess I was just hopin', too. You've got no patent on bein' a jackass, Cash. I thought you ought to know about Yancy not comin'. And I thought you oughta know that, well, I might get after you sometimes, but I'm right proud to stand beside you."

The boy stared at him incredulously. "You are?"

"I am," Dix said with a nod. "Now, let's get back up there. Seems to me we could pull off that stunt again, and maybe this time I could get us some drinkin' water."

Unconsciously, Cash licked his lips. They were parched, what with his losing so much water through sweat, and Dix knew the kids were probably worse off than they were. "And don't put another shot that close to my ear," he said with a smile as they started forward, "or you'll rue the day."

Cash hooted. "Rue the day? What the hell does that mean?"

Dix shrugged. "Read it in a book somewhere."

20

Melody cowered when the shooting started again. Nancy had jumped, but neither child noticed, being occupied by their own fears.

She hugged Melody close. James lay curled on his side, his arms around Papagayo's neck. Through the echoing thunder of gunfire that sent dirt and small rocks sifting from the ceiling, she could hear him comforting the dog.

"It's all right, boy," he soothed over the din as he stroked Papagayo's red-merled coat. It was nearly obscured by mud and dried blood. "Easy, boy." She knew he was comforting himself as much as the dog who, in spite of his wounds and prone position, barked out a steady stream of complaints against the noise.

Melody had both hands over her ears. "Make them stop!" she cried. Nancy just hugged her harder.

And then the gunfire ceased. "Thank God," she whispered, although she couldn't hear herself. Her ears were still ringing. Papagayo stopped his barking and gave his tail a couple of thumps in the mud.

She smiled, just a little. "There," she said, and this time

she could hear her own voice. "Papagayo made them stop."

Melody sprang from her arms and knelt beside the animal. "Oh, good dog!" she cooed, and patted him, carefully avoiding the arrow wounds in his flank and hip before she looked back at Nancy with those wide blue eyes. "Can we go back to the house yet?" she asked. "I'm tired of this game."

"We're all tired and hot, dear," Nancy said patiently. It was an understatement if ever there was one.

Melody frowned and said, "I'm awful thirsty, too."

"I know, baby," Nancy said.

"It's not a game," James piped up, frowning. "Julio and the others are shooting 'cause they have to. And we have to stay here. Remember when Tábano made me do that test?"

Melody shook her head.

"Why, he made me run around the whole camp about fifty times with a mouthful of water, and I couldn't swallow one darn drop! It took all afternoon, but I did it," he added proudly. "And back then I wasn't older than you."

"James!" Nancy said in disbelief, and in shock as well. She had never, until this day, heard James utter one word about his years with the Apaches. "Tábano made you do this?"

He nodded. "It's a test all the Apache boys have to do." He lowered his eyes to the panting dog. "Course, Tábano didn't have me do the whole thing. I wanted to, but he wouldn't let me. He said I was white and soft." He looked up again angrily. "I could've done it all, Nancy."

"Yes," Nancy said, "I believe that you could. You're a strong lad, James, and very brave."

"I'm still thirsty," said Melody, and she crossed her muddy arms with a sharp little sigh.

Suddenly, Papagayo made an attempt to stand, and over

the sounds of James gently coaxing him back down, she heard the approach of boots, accompanied by the soft clunk of mud-clotted spurs. She caught herself smoothing her bodice, then rolled her eyes. She could be such a goose at times!

She rose just as Dix came into the haze of light shed by their lanterns. She'd put her foot down on the primping, but she couldn't hold back the wee smile that bloomed on her face.

"Hello," she said, and a clot of dirt tumbled from her head. And then she noticed that he was carrying a corked pottery jug and two bottles. Her hands went to her throat and she found that she was licking her lips. "You've brought water!"

"Water!" squealed Melody, leaping to her feet, and they all cringed when the high-pitched sound was amplified by the tunnel walls.

"A little less noise, please, lassie," Nancy said, chuckling.

Dix handed each of the children a bottle. Melody drank greedily, pausing only to say, "Next time, could you bring limeade, please?"

James didn't drink. He carefully poured water into his cupped hand and offered it to Papagayo. The dog lapped gratefully, and James filled his hand again.

"Aren't you going to drink?" Dix asked.

"Oh!" Nancy said. "Oh, yes!"

"Sorry about all the commotion," he said as she uncorked the jug and tipped it to her lips. "We had to lay down cover so we could grab the jars and jugs."

Hot water had never tasted so good. Nancy drank and drank, feeling a little like a sponge that had been wrung out hard, then run over by a freight wagon for good measure. She paused only long enough to pour a little into her hand

and splash her face and hairline. When she did, muddy water streamed into her eyes.

Dix simply stood there and watched her, and she thought what a fine impression she must be making on this man. Mud and sweat and soot and a scalp full of dirt, and now here she was, drinking like a plow horse just in from the fields. Well, it could only get better from here.

And then she reminded herself that it might just get worse, first. A great deal worse.

And when Dix began, "Now, if they get in here . . ." her heart sank.

"Or if something happens to us," he continued, "I want the three of you to head down the tunnel. We're deeper than you think, and the water level's not far. You can smell it."

She could. She had even smelled it yesterday, when they were up-tunnel, drinking limeade and eating chicken and thinking that they had it bad. The stench of the water was stronger here, a dank, rotting odor.

She didn't want to think about the creatures that would live in such a black and hopeless pond. Things that swam and skittered, she supposed. Tiny blind fish. And worse, she knew the edges of the water would be thick with sticky black widow webs. She had already killed better than a dozen in their immediate area. At least the children knew not to put a hand anywhere that they hadn't looked first.

"If they come, leave the dog here and get down into that water," Dix continued.

"Leave Papagayo?" asked James pleadingly.

"I'm afraid so, son," Dix said softly. "If they get a gander at his eyes, it might keep them from coming any farther. But if they follow you, Nancy, put your lantern out and swim as far back as you can."

Melody shook her head. "I don't want to go in any water!"

Before Dix or Nancy could speak, James put his hand on Melody's arm. "It's quiet water, Melody," he said softly. "I'll hang on to you. It'll be all right. I promise."

Quite seriously, Dix said, "I'm putting you in charge, James."

The boy looked up and nodded.

Nancy waited for Dix to look at her again, and then she said, "Thank you."

Dix seemed to be struggling with something, for he opened his mouth and then closed it again twice. She waited, and finally he said, "Nancy, there's somethin' I've been meanin' to say to you. It's just . . . well, what I mean to say is that I, uh, I admire . . ."

A single shot rang out, up-tunnel, and they all turned toward it. Cash's voice followed immediately. "They got the last body, Sheriff!" he shouted.

"Aw, shit," Dix swore, then colored slightly. He turned to face Nancy again. "'Scuse me," he said with a tip of his battered hat. "You folks be ready."

And with that, he moved off into the darkness, back up to join the others.

She stood there for a long time, the water jug dangling from her fingers.

Brush began to fall down the hole and onto the mounded dirt in the light, and Dix could do nothing but shake his head.

"I'll bet them sons a bitches are jammin' it down with one'a them boards," Cash said.

"Yeah," said Dix. With every newly uprooted shrub came a heavy spatter of fresh dirt and stones, knocked loose from the sides of the hole. The opening had started out barely large enough for a lean man to wriggle down, but its size was steadily increasing.

"I don't get it," said Cash grumpily. "If they're gonna

set another fire, all the smoke'll just go right up the chimney, won't it?"

The kid still didn't understand. Dix flicked sweat from his brow and said, "Would if they were goin' to leave a chimney, Cash."

Cash's eyebrows bunched together. "Huh?"

"They will close it up," said Julio in explanation. He took another long drink of his water. He'd already emptied the first jar and was working on the second. "They will smoke us like a turkey."

Reason dawned over Cash's face. "Do you have to be so goddamned upliftin' all the time?" he asked angrily.

Three more scrubby bushes momentarily blocked the light, then tumbled down the hole. They rolled off the pile, spraying dirt and dead leaves.

Julio inched up to the light and leaned out as far as he dared. With the barrel of his rifle, he shoved the closest bush away from the pile. This action was greeted with gunfire from above, and two arrows whooshed down to dig deeply into the dirt, mere inches from his fingers. He pulled back, muttering, *"¡Chingate!"*

"Terrific," said Cash. "Now what we gonna do?"

Another bush fell through the opening, scattering leaves and dirt. It was followed directly by the whoosh of an arrow, this one flaming.

Cash yelped, "Crimeny!" and jumped back, but Dix grabbed a couple of the full water jars.

"Julio!" he shouted. The fire was spreading fast, curling dead leaves, racing along twigs, filling the air with smoke.

Julio's rifle was already at his shoulder. *"¡Ándele!"* he shouted.

Dix tossed the first jar high over the growing flames. Julio fired, shattering it in midair. The fire hissed, but it didn't go out.

Dix tossed the second jar. Again, Julio found his mark.

This time, the jar was too far to the side when the slug shattered it, and water splatted against the wall. Dix turned to grab the third and last jar, but Cash was already winding up to toss it.

"Aim good, Julio," the kid said, and lobbed the jar in a gentle arc.

Julio did, and this time the flames died with a sudden hiss.

Grinning, Cash batted at the smoky air. "By gum!" he said.

But Dix frowned. They'd put it out this time, but he knew those Apaches weren't going to quit. He said, "Calm down, boy. That was the end of our drinking water, aside from whatever Julio's got left, and what I took back to Nancy and the kids."

"There is water deeper in the mine," Julio reminded him.

Wearily, Dix nodded. "I know, but we're fresh out of things to carry it in." He took silent stock of his aching muscles, then said, "You're gonna have to cover me one more time, friend. I'm gonna try to get the wash bucket."

"Let me go," said Cash.

Both Julio and Dix turned to look at him.

"I mean it," Cash said, and his features were set. "Seems like you fellers are taking all the chances."

"Seems to me that you're the only one who's taken any arrows," Dix replied. "I swear, boy, you're a real magnet for 'em."

"Yeah, well, them Apaches can't seem to hit me dead center," Cash said, "and at least I'm young and fast. Sheriff, if you had any more hitches in your gitalong, we could put you up for a statue in the town square and let the birds shit on you."

Julio chuckled under his breath.

Dix knew he was sore, all right, but he hadn't known it showed. "Shut up, Julio," he grouched.

"Besides," Cash added, "either one'a you can shoot better than me."

Dix sighed. "All right," he said at last, just as the light from above dimmed, then showed bright again as another uprooted shrub, then two more, came down the hole. He batted at the stray leaves, then drew his gun.

The sound of a gunshot, distant yet distinct, echoed thinly over the plain and carried down the light shaft, down the tunnel.

"Hold on," Dix said, hoping against hope.

"What?" ask Cash, who was poised for his leap into the open.

"Listen."

It came again, closer this time.

Now the gunfire came to them in a staccato pattern. It sounded like popcorn popping over a fire, growing closer all the time.

Julio turned his head toward Dix. "It is your deputy. He has come at last!" just as another flaming arrow sped down into the brush.

21

"Cover me!" Dix shouted, then raced forward into the light, into the rapidly sprouting flames.

The water with which they'd doused the first fire did nothing to impede the second. Dix kicked and batted at waist-high flaming brush. Smoke filled his eyes, his nose, singed his cotton trousers and shirt. Teary-eyed, choking, and deafened by gunfire, he fought the flames on sheer instinct, blindly kicking the scrub apart, beating at flames with his blistering hands.

He felt a hand on his shoulder and turned toward it, swinging blindly, thinking that one of those sons of bitches had somehow climbed down the hole or had come up from the other side of the mound.

But just as his fist connected with flesh, he heard Julio shout, "You are on fire, *señor!*"

He stumbled back, taking the falling form of the man he'd slugged with him, and landed against Julio. Someone pounded at his shirt, his britches, rolled him over and over on the muddy ground. At last his eyes, blurred by smoke and tears, made out Julio.

"The fire!" he half-coughed and tried to get to his feet. Sharp pain seared his arm.

Julio pushed him back down. "Is no matter," he said. "They do not close the hole. Look for yourself."

Dix blinked. Sure enough, the remains of the brush still burned, but the smoke was carried upward and out. He could still hear the rifle fire from outside. He touched his arm, and when he did the pain was so great that he grimaced and fresh tears, this time from the searing pain, sprang to his eyes. "Jesus!" he hissed, and then he remembered the fellow he'd hit, and asked, "Who'd I slug?"

"Who else?" asked Julio. He nodded toward Cash, who was slumped in the mud against the far wall, feeling his jaw and looking painfully annoyed.

"Ouch," Cash said, wincing. He squinted through the thinning smoke at Dix. "Your hat's still smokin'."

Dix grabbed it off his head and beat it out. "Sorry about your jaw," he muttered.

"Least you didn't shoot me with an arrow," Cash said and worked his jaw around. "Had about enough'a those for one day."

Julio had lit the lantern again. "If you have finished with your afternoon social," he said, rising, "maybe we should go and help the men who have come to rescue us."

He rose and crossed through the light, carefully working his way through the burning scrub before anybody could get a shot off to cover him. It didn't matter. No arrows flew down. The Apache braves that had been up top were busy elsewhere. And the Apache who'd been on the other side of the mound had apparently fled.

"Are you going to just sit there?" Julio shouted from across the fire.

"Hell, no!" said Dix, and he climbed to his feet with new vigor. He gave Cash a hand up, and they wove through the fire and crossed the light, too, and followed

Julio up the shaft. He wanted to see just who the devil
Yancy had dug up to help them. He couldn't picture any of
Old Man Peterson's boys laying waste to a place with such
vigor as it sounded like these fellows possessed.

When they came to the bend in the tunnel, Julio
stopped, crouched low, and waved them to do the same.
Dix crawled up next to him just in time to see Julio raise
his rifle again.

Their table barricade had been tossed to one side, and
he had a clear view of the tunnel's mouth. Two braves,
their backs toward Dix, Julio, and Cash, were crouched inside it: one with a rifle, the other with a bow and arrows.
The one with the rifle had the stock against his shoulder,
and he was carefully following distant movement.

Julio fired twice in rapid succession. The brave with the
rifle fell first, followed directly by the one with the bow.

Dix shook his head. He said, "Goddamn. You want a
job?"

Julio picked up the lantern again. *"Gracias, señor,* but I
already have one, if my little goats are still speaking to
me." He moved forward. Dix limped after him, followed
by Cash.

But when they reached the mouth of the mine and its
blessedly cool breeze—by comparison, anyway—Dix
didn't see any townies. Instead, the place was swarming
with Mexicans. And by the way they were armed, they
were bandits.

The rifle fire had all but died by this time, as had the
wind. Riders slowly moved in and out between the smol-
dering buildings the Indians had set aflame in the morning,
and there were more riders across the river. Its floor was
once again reduced to nothing but rocks and debris.
Through the humidity, the air stank of rotting fish and
smoke.

Outside the adobes on the riverfront street, men on foot

patrolled, and an occasional muffled shot issued from inside a building. He watched while two Mexicans dragged a dead Apache from Enrique and Soledad's house and tossed him into the dusty road like so much garbage.

He couldn't see Yancy anywhere.

"You want I should get Nancy and the kids?" Cash asked him.

"You'd best wait," Dix said. "We don't know if these fellas are exactly friendly."

"I don't much care," Cash said with a sigh, and slumped to the ground. "I ain't got the strength to fight off a whole new crew."

Frankly, Dix didn't figure he possessed the strength, either, but he said, "Wait anyway."

Julio was staring out through the dying light, looking over the men, and at last his eyes came to rest on a fellow not too far off, a fellow riding a rangy black bay. *"¡Madre de Dios!"* he whispered. "Can this be Juan?"

And then he stepped out, walking clear of the mine's low shadow, and waved his arms. *"¡Hola!"* he cried. *"¡Amigo!"*

"Hey!" Dix shouted, suddenly panicked. "You don't know who—"

But he stopped in midsentence, because the man swung his rifle wide with a joyous whoop of greeting, and then wheeled his horse and loped toward them. He leapt down before the horse had come all the way to a halt and rushed to Julio, throwing his arms about him.

"¡Mi amigo!" the bandit cried. A handsome man, he was draped in bandoliers and wearing a pirate's smile. "We could not find anyone. We thought you were all dead!" And then he held Julio at arms' length, and a look of surprise, then abject joy, crossed his face. "By the saints! Is this Julio Santiago?"

"It is, you young rascal," Julio replied sternly. "Why have you taken so long to come?"

It suddenly dawned on Dix just who this overarmed character was: Juan Alba. Juan Alba, with a five-thousand-dollar reward on his head.

Alba, who was not paying the least bit of attention to Dix, cocked a brow. "You were expecting me, *Señor* Santiago?"

Cash had climbed back up to his feet, and he whispered, "What the hell's goin' on?" Dix elbowed him in the ribs. To the north, four riders lit out toward the east at a gallop.

"Not you, precisely, Juan," Julio said, smiling. "Just someone like you."

"Ah," said Alba, as if he understood.

"Allow me to introduce to you my comrades," Julio said grandly and swept an arm back toward Dix and Cash. "This is Sheriff Dix Granger, from the town of Gushing Rain, and the young one is Cash Malone, who robbed the bank of that same city. Both the bravest of men."

"Ah, we have something in common," Alba said cryptically. Dix was deciding whether it was a good idea to ask him what he meant, when the Mexican added, "I have seen your deputy this day, Sheriff."

Dix forgot everything else. Stepping forward, he said, "Yancy? Where'd you come across him?"

Alba scratched the back of his neck. "He was on foot, not far from Gushing Rain. He told us of your troubles."

Dix figured it had been a pure miracle that Alba had let him live long enough to say "Good morning," let alone anything else, but he supposed this was a day for miracles.

Of course, if anybody could talk the devil out of his pitchfork, it was Yancy.

Dix said, "Where is he?"

Alba shook his head. "I am sorry to report that one of

my men lost him in the canyon." He brightened. "He is doubtless walking this way."

Dix straightened, despite his throbbing muscles and the pain in his arm. "I'd best ride out for him," he said. "Cash, go back and get Nancy and the kids. And see if you can't get some of her stuff dug out while you're at it."

"There has been a cave-in?" Alba asked, one brow arched. "It was very smart, to hide in this old mine. One entrance, easy to defend."

"That's what *we* thought," Cash muttered at Dix's back. Alba didn't hear him.

"How many men do you need, Sheriff?" Alba said. "To help with the digging."

"Two'd be plenty," Dix replied. They wouldn't need help uncovering the boxes and crates so much as hauling them out, but he didn't feel like explaining it at the moment. "I'm beholden."

"De nada," said Alba with a shrug, then leaned forward, sniffing. He added, "No offense to you, but you stink."

"Don't doubt it," Dix muttered. And then he noticed something glinting on Alba's chest, stuck halfway behind a bandolier: Yancy's badge. Alba saw him looking, and he grinned. He unpinned the badge and handed it over.

"If I had known what a hard job this is," he said, "I would not have wished to wear it. Sitting in the desert like a rock and hiding from Apaches in caves? You who wear badges are the crazy ones."

Cash picked up the lantern and headed back down the mine shaft, and Alba turned again to Julio, saying, "So, Santiago! Tell me of your exploits since the last time we met! How many years has it been?"

That left Dix with nothing to do except limp slowly down to the barn. He hoped Chunk was still there. He hadn't seen any smoke coming from the barn, and that, at least, was a good sign.

He spotted the walking wounded on his way. There were three of the bandits lined up in front of Nancy's house, each one bleeding, but at least they were still standing. A fourth man was digging an arrow out of the arm of one of them, and when it came free and the man let out a tremendous yell, the "doctor" laughed, then splashed it with what Dix supposed was whiskey, because the man hollered again.

The only Apaches he saw were the dead.

Chunk was still in the barn, but a Mexican was with him, just cinching up his saddle. Dix figured he didn't have the time or the strength to dicker with horse thieves. He just walked right up, grabbed the reins, and said, "Thanks."

The Mexican grabbed them back. "Who are you?" he growled, and looked Dix up and down.

"One of the grateful citizens you just saved," Dix replied.

The Mexican made a face. "Your clothes are burnt. And you stink bad."

"Everybody keeps sayin' that."

The Mexican just stared at him, and he was considering drawing his gun and just shooting this son of a bitch, when a thin shouted string of words came to their ears. It was in Spanish, so it was lost on Dix, but the Mexican let go of Chunk's reins and stepped back. He shrugged and, grinning, swept an arm toward the barn doors.

"Andar, Señor Sheriff," he said. "Tell your friend that Tomas says hello."

Dix didn't argue. With no small amount of complaint from his legs, his arms, and his back, he stepped up on Chunk and rode out.

• • •

"You're alive!" Yancy wheezed once Dix brought him back around to consciousness.

It was all but dark, and the shadows were long and deep. It had taken Dix a good bit of time to find Yancy, for he'd fallen into a patch of creosote bushes, which hid him from view. Dix had gone too far north at first, and then backtracked Yancy's faltering footsteps.

"You son of a gun!" Dix exclaimed in relief. "Can you sit up?"

"Reckon," said Yancy, and he heaved himself into a sit. Dix offered him water, and he drank gratefully. At last, he wiped his mouth on his sleeve and asked, "What happened? Did they get there in time?"

"They did," Dix assured him. "How the hell'd you manage to latch on to those *bandidos?* By the way," he said, rifling his pocket, "I got your badge back."

Yancy flushed. "Oh," he said, taking it.

"You'd best keep an eye on that," Dix said. "Must'a cost the city a whole five cents. And where the hell's my horse?"

Yancy pinned on his badge. "Now, Dix, don't get mad."

"Not mad, just askin'. Can you stand up?"

"Yeah, I reckon." He slung an arm around Dix's shoulders and slowly craned himself to his feet. "Remind me to ask you later why you got them half-burnt-up Mexican duds on. And Dasher isn't dead, if that's what you're wonderin'." And then he sniffed the air. "Lord a'mighty! Is that you?"

"Just shut up and get on the horse, will you?" Dix said as the two of them slowly hobbled toward Chunk. "And I wouldn't talk. You stink like creosote."

"Don't know if I want to mount up, exactly, what with you smellin' so rank," Yancy went on. "What'd you do, anyhow? Take a bath in the hog mud?" He sniffed again. "Smoke. And sweat. And somethin' else. Jesus, Dix!" He patted Chunk's neck, whispering, "Glad to see you ain't barbecue, fella."

"They don't have any hogs," Dix said as he put his foot in the stirrup. When he faltered, Yancy gave him a boost, and then Dix hauled Yancy up behind him.

"Sure smells like they do," Yancy muttered.

Dix nudged Chunk with his heels, and they started back toward Regret at a walk. It was nearly dark, but Dix knew the way and the slivered moon was bright and unsheathed by clouds.

"Why didn't you ask that Nancy gal for some perfume or toilet water or somethin'?" Yancy went on. "She looked to me like a woman that'd have some smell-nice stashed away someplace. Mayhap a little drop behind your ears'd cut the—"

"Yancy?" Dix said, cutting him off. "I'm real pleased to find you breathin', but just shut the hell up, all right?"

"Fine," said Yancy. "Just thought you could use a little conversation, that's all. By golly, Dix! How'd you burn your arm so bad?"

"First, tell me how in tarnation you lost my horse."

22

Yancy was sitting out in front of the Gushing Rain jail, his chair leaned back on two legs and propped against the wall, his hat pulled down low over his eyes. He wasn't asleep, just drowsing and thinking about the avalanche of pies and cakes and fried chicken that had been coming in ever since he got back from Regret, and every new batch of food delivered in the arms of a pretty girl.

Life was good.

"Draw, you skunk," growled a sinister voice, and Yancy's chair hit the boardwalk with a thump at the same time he went for his side arm.

"Jesus, Dix!" he grumbled sleepily, once he saw who was standing there. He slid his gun back into its holster. "I didn't recognize you right off with those new glasses. And you're gonna get yourself killed someday. Why, I remember hearin' one time about this fella up along the Platte, got himself shot dead as a post and all because—"

Dix waved his hands, laughing, and Yancy shut up. He

didn't believe that he'd seen Dix laugh so much—or smile so much, for that matter—in all the time he'd known him as he had in these last two weeks.

Still chuckling, Dix said, "All right, Yancy, all right," and sat down in the next chair. He leaned back, took a deep breath, and said, "Some kinda nice mornin', isn't it?"

"If dry heat agrees with you," Yancy groused. "And a scorchin' sun that isn't fit for anything 'cept Gila monsters."

Dix looked up. "Not a cloud in the sky," he said pleasantly.

"And that's another thing. All that damned water we had down south, and not a drop—not one cruddy drop!—got as far as Gushing Rain! I knew all along the town wouldn't see any of it, y'know. Gushing Rain never gets a blessed drop of water."

Dix shrugged his shoulders. "Good travelin' weather, though."

"It is that," Yancy allowed sarcastically. "The whole dang town oughta up and travel right out of here. Dix?"

"Yeah."

"I still don't see why you let Cash go like you did. I mean, givin' him one'a them Indian ponies Alba's boys brought in, then fannin' its butt west!"

Dix smiled and poked his glasses back up his nose. "Yancy, I told you before. If you'd been down that mine with him or caught in that flash flood, you would'a done the same. A boy like that, a boy who just made one dumb mistake over a greedy woman, doesn't need time in Yuma."

"That's what you keep tellin' me. I just don't get it, though. I mean, you been a stickler for the rules ever since I've known you."

"Maybe I stopped being such a stickler," said Dix, still staring up into the sky.

"There's news."

"Maybe, for a change, I decided to go with what was right, and the hell with the rules."

"But you always said as how our job was to just bring 'em in," Yancy went on doggedly. "Let the court decide after that."

"Yancy?"

"Yeah?"

"Stop pickin'."

Yancy heaved a sigh. It wasn't that he really had any argument against what Dix had done. He supposed if anybody deserved a fresh start, it was Cash Malone. He'd surely proved himself down in Regret. At least, he had from what Dix had told him. It was just that he didn't understand what had made Dix change his hard line after so many years.

"All right," Yancy said after a long silence. "I'll let that one pass."

"Big of you," Dix said with a grin.

All this smiling just wasn't natural! Dix didn't look like Dix with that big grin plastered to his face. Combined with the specs, it gave him a whole new look.

Yancy said, "Well, what about Alba? Now, don't get me wrong. I'll keep my mouth shut like we agreed. Hell, I want to keep my job! But Dix," he said, lowering his voice to a whisper, "him and his gang robbed the bank the day after we left! The whole blasted time he was talkin' to me out on the desert—me, wounded, with no horse and a bum leg and soaked to the skin and in dread of my mortal life— he was sittin' there with nine thousand dollars of Old Man Peterson's money in his saddlebags! Why, that money was so fresh and hot, I'm surprised it didn't burn a hole right through the leather!"

"Yeah," said Dix, still smiling. He was looking not at Yancy, and not at the sky, but across the street at Peterson's bank. "You know, I can actually read the letterin' on Peterson's window! Don't know why I didn't get me a pair'a these before. And I thought that the deal with Alba was kind of symmetrical," he said, drawing a circle in the air with his finger. "Didn't you? Besides, did you really expect me to round up fifteen *bandidos* single-handed, and every one of them armed to the teeth?"

"Well . . ."

"And Julio would've pitched in with 'em, I reckon. He was worth any two of them." Dix shook his head in wonder. "Who could have figured that Julio the goatherd was Julio Santiago, the big hero of the Mexican War? I mean, think of the odds!"

Yancy figured that Julio's being a hero sort of depended on which side of the war you'd been fighting on, but he didn't comment. He just said, "Yeah, but at least you could've filed a report."

Dix shrugged. "You want to file one telling all about Alba, go right ahead. There's plenty of forms in the right-hand desk drawer. You do that, and I'll send you a cake with a rasp baked in it, in care of Yuma prison."

Yancy snorted. Dix knew darn well that he'd never file a report, not if his life depended on it. It was just too goddamn embarrassing. Officers of the law having their butts hauled out of the fire by known felons!

"Reckon Julio's all the way to Mexico by now, drinkin' *cervezas* and having a high old time," Dix mused thoughtfully.

Yancy let the change in subject slide. If he never heard Juan Alba's name again, it'd be too soon. Big feet, his butt. He said, "Reckon so. It's a long trip shank's mare, 'specially since he came up here with us first. And 'specially with all those dang goats. What'd he have? Fifteen? Sixteen?"

"More like a dozen," Dix said, looking down the street.

"They just smelled like more. I offered to buy him a horse, but he wouldn't have any of it. The only thing he'd take me up on was a burro to haul his gear. That, and a new hat. Say, Kirk's window says 'Fresh Pies.' I can read it plain. I'll be dogged!"

Yancy fiddled with a crease in his pants leg. "When you leavin'?"

Dix checked his watch. It was a new one that he'd got up at Elsworth's a week past, and it had a little button that, when pushed, played the first few bars of "Lorena."

When Dix had first showed it to him, Yancy'd been sure that Dix was losing his mind. Where was all this sentimental stuff coming from, anyhow? Sentiment and smiling, for God's sake. Nancy's influence, he supposed. A woman surely did make a difference in a man.

"'Bout an hour," Dix said and snapped his watch closed—but not until the watch had finished its tinkly refrain. He smiled at it, then tucked it back into his pocket. "You know, they say all you have to do is throw a little water on it, and that California dirt'll grow just about anything."

"Don't believe everything you hear," Yancy said snidely.

Dix laughed. "I do believe we must have changed places in more ways than one, Yancy. Must've been the badge that did it."

Yancy glanced down at his chest and gave the sheriff's badge a quick polish with his shirtsleeve. Unlike his old deputy's badge, this one was solid silver. "Still don't see why you couldn't stay on. I'd be proud to deputy under you any time, Dix. Provided I got a better grade of badge, of course."

Smiling, Dix shook his head. "I'm done, Yancy. I'm too old for this horse shit. Gonna go to California and grow oranges and lemons and limes and put my feet up every time

I get a chance. They say you have a lot of chances when you grow fruit. Gonna watch those kids grow up, and maybe even have one or two of my own. It's not too late, you know. Nancy's young." He grinned sheepishly. "Well, younger than me."

Yancy just stared at him. Dix had told him before that he was going to farm fruit, but he'd thought Dix was just pulling his leg.

Yancy said, "I knew when you bought that fool watch that you were takin' leave of your senses. You're no dang tree-picker, Dix, you're a lawman!"

"I was only a lawman because I didn't know how to do anything else. Maybe I do now." Dix stood up and stretched his arms. "Well, I'd best get back to the hotel and help Nancy with the packin'. We'll stop by on our way out of town."

Yancy watched as Dix made his way down the sidewalk. He was still short, still had a face that looked like ten miles of bad road, but there seemed to be a spring in his walk that Yancy hadn't noticed until just recently. Nancy had put it there, he supposed. Nancy and Melody and James. He'd never seen a man so foolish over children as Dix was over those two.

Nancy the most. Dix's eyes lit up every time he spoke her name.

But Dix had remained true to form in at least one thing. He'd quit his job quietly, got married quietly, and now he was leaving town quietly. He was even quiet in his joy.

"Must be powerful nice," Yancy muttered to himself as he leaned back in his chair once again. It must be past amazing to feel that way over a woman, to feel that way over kids that weren't even your own.

He closed his eyes as a slow, satisfied smile spread across his face. If anybody deserved to be that happy, albeit quietly, he guessed Dix did.

• • •

"Everything secure?" Dix asked as he tied Dasher's lead rope to the back of the wagon. The horse had taken quite a tumble, but two weeks of rest had put him right as rain, save for the skinned place on his hip, and that was healing nicely. Dasher was no cart horse, though. He'd make the journey trotting along behind the wagon, carrying nothing but his own saddle. Dix had bought a team to pull the wagon, a sturdy pair of plain bay geldings named Roman and Joe.

James shifted the last small box into place and tucked it safely behind a snug rope, then grinned up at him. "Yessir! Secure!"

Dix tousled the boy's yellow hair. "Well, climb on up, and let's get this show on the road!"

Dix waited while James clambered up into the rear seat and squirmed into place beside Melody. Papagayo sat between them, his tail thumping the boards. Before Julio left, he and Dix had decided the boy needed the dog. Besides, Julio had said that after better than a year of being barked at and nipped and worried, his goats would enjoy the peace and quiet. Papagayo would probably limp for the rest of his life, but he was alive and happy. Those were the important parts.

Dix climbed onto the front bench and gave Nancy's hand a squeeze, and she smiled at him. He grinned back. It had taken him a whole week of hemming and hawing and trying to find just the right words, and finally he'd just gone and bought a ring. She'd cried when he got down on one knee, offering the gold band—and not incidentally, himself—and damned if her tears didn't make him cry, too. It was a good kind of cry, though, one he wasn't ashamed of. They'd been married the next day.

And he'd realized, on the first morning of his married life, that he'd at long last put the ghosts of Ramona and

Clara behind him. Nancy had said something to him, back there when they were all huddled up in that mine. She'd said, "Life goes on and drags us along with it," or some such. She had battled past her ghosts, and he found that her kind and solid presence allowed him to do the same. He blessed the day he'd found her.

He picked up the reins.

"We're stopping to say good-bye to Yancy, aren't we?" said Nancy.

"Yes, ma'am," he announced happily, and clucked to the horses. "Get up there, Roman! Get up, Joe!"

Dix whoaed the horses three and a half blocks later. Yancy was still sitting outside, his hat pulled low over his eyes, but he came to attention when the wagon pulled up. A smile splitting his face, he stood up, tipped his hat, and said, "My, my! You two newlyweds off to see the elephant?"

"Are there elephants in California?" Melody asked, wide-eyed. The child was a joy. Everything was brand-new and shiny to her. Nancy had done her hair in braids threaded with pink ribbons today.

"Aw, it's just an expression, silly," James said with a seasoned roll of his eyes.

James had come a very long way in a short period of time. It pleased Dix no end.

Nancy reached across Dix and waved a small envelope at Yancy. He came forward, still limping slightly, and took it, looking up at her with a question on his face.

"Where we'll be moving to," she explained. "My first husband bought the land. Now it's mine. Ours." She touched Dix's elbow, and he took her hand and pulled it through his arm.

"It's supposed to be perfect for fruit," she went on. "Our door is always open to you, Yancy. I do hope you'll come to visit us. You'd be welcome as ice in summer."

"I'd be right pleased to, ma'am," Yancy said with a tip of his hat and a faint blush—Dix guessed that his Nancy just had that effect on a fellow—and tucked the envelope carefully into his pocket.

"Dix," Yancy said, looking up again, "I reckon I don't know what to say. Least you won't be around to shoot me in the butt no more."

Dix chuckled. "Reckon you'll have to find yourself a new deputy," he said. "You can shoot him in the butt yourself."

Grinning, Yancy tipped his head to one side. "I believe I'd admire that."

"Be seeing you, Sheriff," Dix said. Then he turned toward Nancy: his beloved, his wife, his future. "Everybody ready?"

Nancy gave his arm a squeeze, and the children whooped and the dog barked.

"All right, then!" he said, grinning the grin that had seemed to be permanently affixed to his face since they left Regret. He couldn't help it. Life was suddenly too full of joy to frown. To the sound of the children's cheers, he rattled the reins over the horses' rumps.

"Git up, Roman!" he called. "Walk on, Joe!" And they drove on, into the west, into the land of hopes and dreams and bright, shining promise.

No one knows the American West better.

JACK BALLAS

❏ *THE HARD LAND*

0-425-15519-6/$4.99

❏ *BANDIDO CABALLERO*

0-425-15956-6/$5.99

❏ *GRANGER'S CLAIM*

0-425-16453-5/$5.99

The Old West in all its raw glory

PETER BRANDVOLD

❑ ONCE A MARSHAL   0-425-16622-8/$5.99

The best of life seemed to be in the past for ex-lawman Ben Stillman. Then the past came looking for him...

    Up on the Hi-Line, ranchers are being rustled out of their livelihoods...and their lives. The son of an old friend suspects that these rustlers have murdered his father, and the law is too crooked to get any straight answers. But can the worn-out old marshal live up to the legendary lawman the boy has grown to admire?

❑ BLOOD MOUNTAIN   0-425-16976-6/$5.99

Stranded in the rugged northern Rockies, a wagon train of settlers is viciously savaged by a group of merciless outlaws rampaging through the mountains. But when the villains cross the wrong man, nothing on Earth will stop him from paying every one of them back—in blood.

> "Make room on your shelf of favorites:
> Peter Brandvold will be staking out a claim
> there." —Frank Roderus